P9-BVM-721

The Magic Stone

Leonie Kooiker

Illustrated by Carl Hollander

Translation from the Dutch
by Richard and Clara Winston

William Morrow and Company
New York 1978

Originally published in the Netherlands
under the title *De heksensteen*
by Uitgeverij Ploegsma, Amsterdam.

Inquiries should be addressed to
William Morrow and Company, Inc.,
105 Madison Ave., New York, N. Y. 10016.

Library of Congress Cataloging in Publication Data
Kooiker, Leonie.
The magic stone.
Summary: Chris finds a magic stone
and becomes the focus of interest
for an association of witches, one of whom
wants him to become her successor.
[1. Witchcraft—Fiction. 2. Witches—Fiction]
I. Hollander, Carl. II. Title.
PZ7.K83557Mag [Fic] 78-1713
ISBN 0-688-22143-2 ISBN 0-688-32143-7

Printed in the United States of America.
First Edition
1 2 3 4 5 6 7 8 9 10

To my friend Hein, without whom
this book would never have been written,
and to the real Chris.

Contents

CHAPTER I

The Wheelchair

Chris had been given a box of little plastic thingamajigs, and now he was making a model ship out of them. There was a diagram that showed how all the pieces fitted together, and when you glued them all, you had a ship. It was finicky work. Chris didn't really mean to spend a lot of time on it, but he was eager to see what the ship would look like when it was finished. So he couldn't very well stop now. He wanted to have a ship like this one for real when he grew up. Also a huge house in a forest. No reason why not, for he intended to be rich someday. As yet he did not know exactly what he was going to be, but at any rate he would do something you could make an awful lot of money at.

Chris lived with his parents and sister in a suburb. There was a lot of talk about money in their household, mostly about the fact that there was not enough of it. Chris thought that was a bore, and he also thought his father was rather stupid for not having chosen a different line of work. He himself meant to look around a lot more carefully. And he would have a big barn of a house, not with a silly pocket-sized garden but with woods all around it. Having all sorts of wild animals living in the woods would be just fine, since he wouldn't be afraid of them. It was convenient, being that way. He was just never scared of anything, neither of wolves nor swooping owls. He wasn't even scared of big fat spiders, or of the dark, or of the police.

"Chris," his mother said, "do you hear me?"

"Yes."

"We'll be going away for a few days."

"Oh? Us children too?"

"No, just Father and I. You can choose where you'd like to stay."

"How many days?"

"Four. Johanna will be going to Granny's, and you can stay with Jim or Kees or Paul."

"I don't want to stay with Jim or Kees or Paul. I want to stay with Frank."

"With Frank? Why?"

"That will be more fun."

"You play with Paul much more often."

"Still, I want to stay with Frank."

"But I don't know Frank's mother so well. I thought . . . ."

"Should I go and ask her myself?"

"Oh, no. I'll ask, since you'd rather stay with Frank. But what's the idea?"

"I just think I'll have more fun. I told you that."

"You don't have some mischief up your sleeve?"

"Of course not. You don't understand about that. Mischief isn't something you plan on beforehand. It always happens by accident. First I do something, and later on I realize it was mischief. And anyhow Frank is a quiet sort of fellow."

"Yes," Mother said, "that's true enough."

She gazed thoughtfully at Chris, who was gluing a thin railing along the side of his ship with the utmost finickiness and calm. Then she left the room, and Chris picked up the next piece of railing.

I said that well, he thought. That was a neat little fib.

For Chris very definitely meant to get into mischief at Frank's house. He had had something in mind for a good long time. And he had fibbed so cleverly that it almost amounted to a lie. Chris was highly pleased with himself.

With great precision and care he fitted the railing

into its place, meanwhile considering how he was going to bring Frank around to helping out.

Frank was a scaredy-cat sometimes.

Frank's house was a few blocks away. It was somewhat smaller than Chris's and a good deal darker. Frank had a brother and sister, both older than himself, and his grandmother lived upstairs. Chris also had a grandmother, but she was just an ordinary old lady. Frank's grandmother was more like the real thing.

Chris had seen her only a few times. Each time he had stared at her in that cheeky way of his and noticed everything about her: her wrinkled little face, her really snow-white hair, and the black dress that was a lot longer in front than behind. That was because she walked crookedly. Frank's grandmother needed two canes to walk around the house, and outside she didn't walk at all. She used a wheelchair. It stood in the hall in Frank's house, dreadfully in the way because the place was cramped enough as it was.

And this was the mischief Chris had dreamed up: he wanted to go for a ride in Frank's grandmother's wheelchair. It had a pair of huge wheels, much bigger than bike wheels, and a small wheel in the front. The wheelchair was operated by a pair of handles that you moved up and down. There was a kind of pouch for the feet, made of rough black cloth; it could be closed with snaps.

The wheelchair was the oddest vehicle Chris had ever seen, and he imagined it would be terrific fun to ride it down the street and go whooshing around the curves.

Frank and he would both fit comfortably in it together. They would both have to pull very hard on those crazy handles, and of course they'd tire quickly if they drove it fast. They'd have to take the wheelchair out on the sly, of course. But that wasn't too hard, because Frank's grandmother sat upstairs all day long. They would just wait until Frank's mother went out. His father always came home late, and so did his brother and sister.

Actually, there was no reason to worry even if they were caught at it. They might be given a scolding, but if they were careful not to break anything it wouldn't be so bad. After all, a contraption like that had to be used now and then. Wheels that are never used get stiff and squeaky. They might as well oil the wheelchair. Frank's grandmother would surely be pleased if they took care of that for her.

And after all, if they oiled it they had to take it out and test drive it.

* * *

Frank's mother agreed to have Chris stay for four days, and so on Thursday he did not return home from school, but went along with Frank.

It was odd, kind of like setting out in the wrong direction.

Mother had brought Chris's suitcase to Frank's house. It was already sitting in the attic room. Frank always slept in the attic, and so did Chris now. It was jollier than his own room at home. Frank was allowed to paste or tack anything he liked to the boards of the slanting roof, and he had put up all kinds of stuff. And the floor was enormous. There was plenty of room to play with cars and trains. Only one thing was a bit tiresome: they had to be quiet. On account of Frank's grandma. Frank always called her "grandmother."

"Under here is my grandmother's room. You always have to be careful not to irritate her. If she gets offended, you're in trouble."

"What does she do?" Chris wanted to know. But Frank did not answer.

"She's awfully nice when she isn't offended."

They played quietly with Frank's fleet of automobiles, and Chris did not dare to broach the matter of the wheelchair. What if Frank's grandmother could hear through the floor?

He didn't bring up the subject until the next day, on

the way home from school. "Have you ever ridden in your grandmother's wheelchair?"

Frank looked stunned. This was something he had never thought of.

"How fast can it go?" Chris asked. "Do you think it would go as fast as a moped if you rode it downhill on Mozart Street?"

Frank was still looking staggered. "Grandmother never goes in that direction. When she goes anywhere, it's always into town."

"Does she go out often?"

"Hardly ever."

Chris nodded. He had thought as much.

"Who oils it when it squeaks?"

"It doesn't squeak. Never has."

"How do you know, if she hardly ever takes it out?"

By now they had reached Frank's house. The front door was locked, of course. Frank didn't ring; he went down a narrow lane alongside the next house and so reached the back door. That was never locked. In the kitchen stood a tray with two glasses of lemonade and a bowl of crackers. There was a note by the tray: "I've gone to the dentist. Will be home around five. Mother."

It was very quiet in the house. Grandmother was undoubtedly still asleep. She took an afternoon nap every day.

"You know, I have oil," Chris said. "From my bike

kit. I've got it right with me. Don't you think we ought to see whether the wheelchair does squeak?"

He went to the front hall and Frank silently followed.

Carefully Chris moved the wheelchair back and forth in the hall. It did not squeak.

"It rides hard," Chris said. "It needs oiling."

"You better leave it alone," Frank said. "If my grandmother gets offended, you're in trouble."

"There's no way to tell whether it squeaks until you ride it on the street, because the floor here is too level. And we can't oil it here either because we might spill some oil on the rug. But if we oil it outside and it runs easily, your grandmother's going to be awfully pleased. How long does she nap in the afternoon? Till when?"

"If anyone touches her things, she's wide awake right away."

"She won't notice anything."

"She sure will. She always does."

"I don't believe it. Want to bet?"

"No."

"Scared?"

"No."

"If you don't dare to bet, you're scared."

By now Chris had pushed the wheelchair right up to the front door. The handles went up and down of their own accord.

"Terrific vehicle," Chris said.

Frank began to laugh when one of the handles just missed Chris's head. Chris started laughing too.

"Come on, let's try it," Chris said. "Open the door."

And Frank did, very cautiously. Together they tugged at the wheels to lift the heavy thing over the threshold, and by the time Frank very quietly closed the front door Chris was already in the wheelchair.

"Wait," Frank said. "I want to ride too."

They were able to sit side by side on the seat. Each one gripped a handle tightly. Up, down, up down; when Frank's handle went up, Chris's went down. It wasn't at all hard. The wheelchair did not need oiling.

"Right turn," Chris said. "We'll coast down Mozart Street."

And Frank, who sat on the side with the brake, extended his right arm to indicate the direction of their turn. They whooshed around the curve. Here was a street full of shops.

"We don't want to run over anybody," Frank said.

"We won't," Chris replied, as he swung the chair in a loop around a fat woman trundling her shopping cart.

"Hey, do you have a driver's license?" a man called out, laughing.

But another said, "Watch where you're going, you scamps."

And Chris shouted back cheerily, "What a way to talk to my handicapped little brother!"

It was great fun. They had to make another right turn when they came to Mozart Street. The houses were set back behind small gardens. Here there was little traffic and for a while not a single side street, but the end of the street sloped very steeply.

"Now pull," Chris cried, "pull as hard as you can, and when we reach the slope we'll let her rip. I'll bet she'll go thirty or thirty-five. Don't you think she'll make thirty-five?"

Frank said nothing. He was pumping away at his handle with both hands, his face red from the exertion.

"Let go!" Chris cried.

They crouched down in the seat while the handles whizzed up and down above their heads and the wheelchair rushed down the slope.

"Man," Frank said, "she'll do sixty easy."

For a long way the wheelchair coasted, but then Frank began to brake it, for he did not like the idea of ending their ride by plunging into the water of the canal. They came to a stop by a tall hedge. There was a post with a little sign on it, and Frank gave a start when he noticed it.

"The dentist. This is where the dentist lives. Suppose my mother sees us. How late is it getting to be?"

As he spoke they heard a door open and shut, and

footsteps approached from behind the hedge. Appalled, they stared at each other. Frank's mother had gone to the dentist. Perhaps she was coming out just now.

Frank tore open the snaps of the pouch over their legs and ran away as fast as he could.

It can't be five yet, Chris thought, but for safety's sake he slid down into the pouch. Huddled up, he sat on the footrest, concealed by the ugly black cloth.

He was sitting on something hard. A stone. He adjusted his position so that he was somewhat more comfortable and without thinking thrust the stone into his pocket. Then he froze, still as a mouse. It isn't Frank's mother, he thought; she's probably still sitting in the waiting room, or the dentist is busy right now drilling a deep hole in one of her molars. The footsteps passed by. Chris crawled out and looked around for Frank.

Even if she comes out right now and sees us, Chris thought, we'll just say it was a thief took it. When we came home from school we were just in time to see a big fellow with a checked cap riding off in Grandmother's wheelchair.

There was Frank. Chris rode slowly over to him.

"Listen, Frank, there was a thief."

"Where?" Frank asked.

"No, not a real one, but that's what we'll say. We'll coast downhill once more, and if we meet your mother we'll say that the wheelchair was stolen and that we were just in time—"

"Oh, come on," Frank said, "she won't believe a word."

"How about trying Beethoven Street? There isn't much traffic there either."

But Frank was scared and wanted to go home.

"Listen, it's stupid to go home now. This is our big chance. Do you think your mother's going to have an appointment with the eye doctor tomorrow?"

"I think Grandmother must be awake by now, and if she finds out she'll be offended."

"I guess you're scared of your grandmother."

"I am."

Chris sometimes put on his own grandmother's hat and pranced around with it, but his grandmother just laughed. He could not imagine that anyone would think it was so awful to take a little ride in this splendid wheelchair. They hadn't broken anything. Stupid Frank, scared of such a wizened old lady. It might have been more fun if he'd stayed with Paul.

Quietly they rode back to Frank's house. It was OK, but nothing happened to make them laugh.

Frank went down the lane to open the door. They put the wheelchair back exactly in its place and then went to the kitchen, where the lemonade was still waiting for them. It was perfectly quiet in the house. Nobody had noticed anything.

They played outside until suppertime, and Chris began to wonder whether Grandmother would be offended as Frank had predicted. But Grandmother didn't even come downstairs.

"She's not quite herself today," Frank's mother said, and she carried a large tray upstairs.

"It isn't because I'm here, is it?" Chris asked.

"Why of course not, my dear, don't worry about that."

But Chris couldn't help wondering, and later in the evening, when he lay in bed next to Frank, he began asking all sorts of questions. Did Grandmother stay upstairs often? How old was she anyhow? How long had she had the wheelchair?

And Frank answered all his questions in whispers. Grandmother had had an accident about ten years ago when she was using a broom to sweep out the gutters along the roof. She'd fallen from the roof, and she was already so old that the doctor had said she would never mend. But all the same she could walk pretty well now. She needed the wheelchair only when she went a considerable distance.

And she almost never stayed upstairs. She wanted to be in on everything, and she meddled in everything.

Yesterday, too, she had been unusually quiet, so maybe Chris did have something to do with it. But it was just as well if she were not quite herself because otherwise she would certainly have noticed about the wheelchair, and Frank was dead certain that then she would have been awfully offended.

Chris still couldn't imagine that irritating your grandmother could be so terrible. He went on thinking about her, and long after Frank was asleep he could still see the fragile old lady who had sat at the table last night saying nothing, but whose fierce eyes constantly darted back and forth at everyone—at Chris too. And now something was the matter with her? Chris wondered whether she was so old that she was almost ready to die. He didn't know much about that. Did old people just die of their own accord, or did they have to get sick first? It would really be something if he happened to be here just when Frank's grandma died.

If that happened, would a coffin be lugged up the stairs, or would they carry Grandmother down, stiff as a salt cod? Chris knew that much about it. Dead people became stiff. Chris would rather have liked to see it. And it wouldn't be so bad for such an awfully old woman to die at last. Then Frank wouldn't have to be afraid of her getting offended and making trouble. Or would it scare Frank if she were carried downstairs all stiff? It was such a drag when a fellow was scared of every little thing.

Grandmother did not die. Next evening she came downstairs again. It was a Saturday and everybody was home.

Frank's mother had made coffee and chocolate milk and baked two big cakes. Some visitors came, a thin woman with black hair and a man with a head shiny as a mirror, without a hair on it. At home Chris always ducked out of sight when strangers came, but here he stayed at the table because the cake was delicious and maybe he'd get another piece. And besides, the bald man told funny stories about a trip he had taken. Grandmother seemed to be enjoying herself thoroughly.

CHAPTER II

Miracles

As the boys were on their way home from school Monday afternoon, Chris kept hoping that Frank's mother would be out again. He would have liked to take one more ride in the wheelchair. But he said nothing about it, since they might not have the opportunity anyhow. And that was how it turned out. His own mother was there to collect him.

"Oh," Chris said, "I thought you weren't coming back till this evening."

His mother laughed. "I guess you've had a good time here. You don't have to come with me if you don't want to."

"But I do. I'll get my suitcase. It's almost packed."

Chris dashed up the two flights of stairs. Halfway

up he suddenly thought, Oh, better be quiet, Grandmother. That was the one trouble with this house. Otherwise he'd had a good time. They had played lots of games with the whole family, which never happened at home, and his idea about the wheelchair had worked out all right, although they'd really just barely sampled it. But his mother never minded the noise no matter how hard he tramped on the stairs at home, and for that reason it was nicer at home than here.

Chris crammed his things into the suitcase. He even remembered to take his toothbrush from the bathroom. But after he had said his thanks all around and bidden everyone good-bye, he nearly went out the door without his jacket. Frank remembered it.

"Oh, yes, my jacket. I haven't had it on all this time except for the first day."

"What's this in your jacket pocket?" Mother asked. "An oil can? Why ever did you take oil with you?"

"Oh, I just did," Chris said. "You never know when you'll need it."

At home he had to tell about what he had done, and his sister did too. She pretended that she had had ever so many more adventures than Chris, but that wasn't so. She told stories about nothing at all. Finally Mother told about her experiences. She had gone along to a small village and had helped Father with his work. Chris's father had an unusual job. He often went traveling, and he would come back with a whole lot of cans of sand that he had taken from rivers and brooks. Later the sand would be washed and sifted and examined under a microscope. There would be a million or so little teeth in the sand, and that way Chris's father knew what animals had lived there in the past. Since he also knew a lot about animals that are living now, it was always fun to go with him. When Chris and Johanna had been small, they had gone on such expeditions. Now they were at school and couldn't go anymore.

"It was a lovely place," Mother said. "There was a little brook with a tiny waterfall and enormous woods. I did a lot of walking."

"Yes," Chris said, "and then you came to a meadow in the middle of the woods, a meadow with very tall grass and a white fence, and a horse came up to you."

"My goodness, Chris, how did you know that?" Mother asked.

"I imagined I saw it," Chris said. "But I can't have because I wasn't there. Fantastic! I don't know myself how I knew it. But that's how it was, right?"

"Yes, that's how it was. He was such a sweet horse. Next day I went there again, and he ran across the whole meadow to come up to the fence. I stroked his forehead, and he gave me such an intelligent look."

"And I knew it," Chris said.

"Yes, you knew it. That's a miracle."

"What fun, a miracle," Chris said, highly pleased, and gave the matter no more thought. Until another miracle happened.

The next miracle came at school a few days later. They were going over a lesson they'd already had. Chris thought that was annoying, and so he was bored. First he rolled his pencil across his desk, and then he began writing a note to Jim.

"Chris," the teacher said, "are you paying attention?"

"Yes, sir," Chris said, and the teacher went on writing on the blackboard. Chris went on with his note. Just in time he noticed that the teacher was coming toward him with big strides. He crammed the note into his pocket and put on an innocent face.

"I've had enough of your monkey business," the teacher said.

"Yes, sir," Chris said. But to himself he thought, Monkey yourself! I wish you'd climb up on the roof.

Then something very peculiar happened. The teacher was still standing in the same spot, but the expression on his face changed. He hunched his shoulders and looked at the piece of chalk in his hand with a stupid grin. Suddenly he bit off a piece and spat it out. Then he walked unsteadily to the window and climbed out through it.

A monkey, Chris thought, he's behaving like a monkey. It was a horrible sight. The class looked stunned. The teacher went and sat down on the ground in the middle of the school yard. He began picking up pebbles and tossing them.

Oh, Chris thought, how ghastly. I didn't really mean it when I wished he was a monkey. In a minute he'll be climbing up on the roof, and if he falls it will be my fault. Please, please come back to normal.

But now his wishing didn't help. Bent over, arms waving wildly, the teacher began to run.

Marleen began to cry. The other children whispered excitedly, "He's gone crazy. The teacher's gone crazy. What's he going to do next?"

No, no, Chris thought. I don't want that, I don't want that. I don't want the teacher to be a monkey. He's a nice man, and I was being naughty just now. It isn't fair for things to happen just because you think them. In despair, he looked around. Frank was staring at him. Frank mustn't think that he, Chris, could do anything about it. He couldn't do a thing. He looked outside again. The teacher had gone to sit down on a bench. He was wiping his face with a handkerchief and no longer looked crazy. Thank goodness that was over.

The door opened and the teacher from across the hall came in. "What's going on here?" she asked.

There was a sudden silence in the room.

"Willem, where is your teacher?"

At that moment their teacher came back, not through the window but from the hallway, just as he usually did. He looked very pale but otherwise seemed normal.

"I'm back," he said, with an appreciative nod to the other teacher.

She returned to her own classroom.

"We'll go on to arithmetic now," their teacher said. He wiped the board clean and began writing down some tough examples. "Work these out on scrap paper first."

The whole class set eagerly to work. Chris tried hard to do his best, but his mind kept going over what had happened.

I really couldn't have known, could I? It isn't right for everything you think to happen, and it's not much fun either.

After a while the thought occurred to Chris that under certain circumstances it might be fun for things to happen when you imagined them. On the way home from school he started thinking up examples. For instance, wouldn't it be fun if licorice candy came out of the air? Under his breath he said, "I want it to rain licorice."

It didn't work at all. Maybe that was the wrong kind of wish. He had to make somebody do something. Chris looked around for somebody. There was a baker.

I want the baker to give me a currant bun. He looked fixedly at the baker and thought hard about a currant bun. But the man merely said hello to him and turned in at the next gate. Again it hadn't worked. How was he supposed to go about it? Once again he thought over how he'd known so exactly what the meadow looked like where his mother had met the horse. What had he done then? Nothing. He had been thinking of the times when he and Johanna had been taken on the trip, and he had been wishing that he had been along. But just now he had also wished hard for a currant bun . . . . So when a miracle happened, it came unexpectedly. That was the only way Chris could understand it.

At home, he went straight to his room. He stood at the window looking out, hands in his pockets, and felt the wad of paper—the note he had been writing to Jim when the miracle happened. He also felt a pebble. Chris took it out. It was the pebble he had found in Frank's grandmother's wheelchair. It had been in his jacket pocket, but at some time or other he must have stuck it into his trousers pocket.

For the first time Chris took a good look at it. It was somewhat smaller than a marble and not round, but flat. In color it was black or dark green. But no, now it looked dark red. The color seemed to depend on how he held it. There was a star inside it. When he held it up to the light in a certain way, he distinctly saw a five-pointed star. It was a handsome stone. Maybe Frank's grandmother had lost it out of a ring, or something like that. Probably she would be glad to have it back.

Chris placed it cautiously on the table. Then he went hunting for a matchbox. He took a wad of absorbent cotton from the bathroom, carefully packed the stone in the cotton, then placed it in the matchbox, and put the box deep in the drawer of his desk. He wanted to hang on to the pretty stone for a while longer.

On the following days no more miracles happened.

"Will you come to my house to play this afternoon?" Frank asked.

"Sure."

Chris thought of the stone in his desk drawer. He really ought to take it with him. It wasn't his, and he ought to take it back to Frank's grandmother, who had lost it. But then again there was time enough for that. She might not even be home today.

She was, though. When he was going upstairs with Frank, on the way to the attic, her door suddenly opened. She stood very quietly and looked at him. Chris was never scared of anything. But this time he almost was; he simply could not say a word. And then he realized that he could not move either. He seemed to be paralyzed. A feeling of panic swept over him. He wanted to run away, out of the house, and never come back again. But this feeling did not last long. Then Chris grew furious. That ugly old witch! Did she think she could push him around? Let her try it. Let her try scaring him and chasing her grandson's friend out of the house. Nasty hag.

But he wouldn't let himself be chased, and he wouldn't let himself be paralyzed. He was on his way upstairs to play with Frank and that was where he was going. Chris tugged and tugged at his feet, which would not obey. He looked back at Grandmother as fiercely as he could, and suddenly she turned around and went back into her room, leaning on her two canes, pitiably thin, with high shoulders and a thin old back.

The boys went on, up the next flight. Chris dropped down on Frank's bed. He could not help sighing deeply.

"She only does that kind of thing when she's offended," Frank said. "It's pretty uncomfortable, and that's why I didn't like doing—what we did. Do you understand now?"

"Yes," Chris said. "But she didn't see us, or did she?"

"I don't know. I don't think she knows just what we did, but she knows that something happened. That's why you had to come this afternoon."

"You mean she wanted me to come?" Chris forgot to whisper.

"Quiet," Frank said. "I couldn't help it. You've seen that for yourself. What did she ask you?"

Ask? Chris was feeling more and more confused. Not a word had been spoken there on the stairs. That was what made the whole thing so upsetting.

"She usually does that when she wants to know something," Frank said. "She thinks about something, and then she puts it into your head too. You just can't help thinking about it. For instance, if she had made me think about the wheelchair, I would have had to think about you right away and about the dentist's shingle. And then she would be onto the whole thing."

"That's impossible," Chris said. "You can't put things into other people's heads." But even as he spoke he remembered how he had seen the meadow with the black horse, and what had happened at school. The teacher had acted like a monkey, and Chris was the one who had made him do that.

"She can," Frank said. "And she can make you do things too. Once my brother had to sit in his room for two days because she was punishing him. And the door was open all the time."

"It's pretty mean of her to do such things," Chris said.

"She isn't mean at all. She knows a lot more than

we do. Whenever she does that sort of thing she always has a reason for it. At least my mother says so. And we're fond of her, too."

"I'd never be fond of anybody like that," Chris said. "And if I were your mother I'd get rid of her. I'd put her in an old-ladies' home. Or make her stay in her room alone for two days—or for two years. That would be even better."

He slid off the bed and picked up one of Frank's army trucks. "Want to play war? Blow up the railroads?"

"No," Frank said.

"You know what I did once? Tied a firecracker behind a locomotive. It went like the wind, but it got kind of bashed in. I guess we can't do anything like that here, can we? Too much of a racket."

"Yes," Frank said. "And I'd rather not have my locomotive smashed."

"Mine was just an old one. Though my mother was pretty mad about it. The mark on the floor still shows."

"You always want to play such wild games. Don't you like the ordinary ones?"

"Yes, sometimes. Ordinary ones sometimes and wild ones other times. That's the way I like it. And right now I want something wild because your grandmother paralyzed me on the stairs and I'm peeved at her. But I see it won't do. So all right, let's play ordinary."

Chris stayed a few hours playing quietly in the attic with Frank. When it was time to go home, he felt full of suspense and waited to see whether anything new would happen on the stairs. But Grandmother's door remained shut. He did meet somebody on the stairs, however: a tall man in a wide, dark cape. He had bushy eyebrows that almost hid his eyes.

"She's sent for the doctor," Frank said.

"Mother," Chris asked, "do witches and wizards exist?"

"No, dearest, they don't exist."

"And magic—does that really exist?"

"No, you know that."

"Yes, but when you were telling us about the woods and then I knew about the horse, that was a kind of magic, wasn't it? You yourself said it was a miracle."

"That's true. It was very strange. Have you had more such experiences?"

"No, I just wanted to know whether there are real witches."

"In olden days people thought there were, and I suppose it's possible that in those times there were people who could do things that were beyond ordinary people. That even may be so nowadays. But most of the time such things happened unexpectedly and not very often. On the other hand, you might call the telephone or television a kind of magic. You turn a knob and you see or hear something that is happening on the other side of the world. That really is a sort of magic."

"I suppose . . . ."

It was hard. Chris did not want to tell his mother everything he had experienced. In the first place nobody knew about his little ride in the wheelchair. And in the second place he had an idea that everything was connected with the stone he was still keeping hidden in his room. Maybe, without even knowing it, he had aimed one of the rays of the star at his mother, and later at the teacher, while the stone was in his pocket. Grandmother had lost the stone. For that reason she had not been able to direct questions to him on the stairs in the way Frank described. And now she couldn't keep Frank's brother a prisoner in his room or take action when she was offended. Come to think of it, it was a good thing she no longer had that stone.

All very well for Mother to say there was no such thing as magic, but at any rate there must be such a thing as a wicked witch, and Frank's grandmother was one. Chris felt sure of that now. He would see to it that she never got her magic stone back. Chris could use it himself. He would try putting a spell on Johanna sometime. That would be fun.

CHAPTER III

The Little Cafe

Chris was bicycling into town, bound for his trumpet lesson. Mother had taken him there for his first lesson. Then he had gone by streetcar a few times. But that took a terribly long time because he had to transfer. Now at last he was being allowed to go alone, which suited him fine. It was no more dangerous than riding to school on his bike, although it was lots farther. When he rode back, it would be a quarter to five and traffic would be heavy. It was fairly heavy right now, for that matter. Chris kept properly close to the curb, his trumpet behind him, and cars passed close by at his side. A short distance in front of him something was slowing traffic, and cars had to keep swinging out to pass it. Sometimes they could not, and then the whole lane stopped.

The thing up front looked rather like a three-wheeled delivery vehicle, but not quite. What could that black thing with big wheels be? Why, it was more like Grandmother's wheelchair! Chris pedaled somewhat faster.

Sure enough, there she was. She was wearing an odd black hat with her small bun of hair sticking out at the back. Chris felt himself growing more and more excited. Grandmother was going into town. What for? Maybe she was on her way to a gathering of witches? Should he follow her? It was still early. He had time to see where she was going and still make his trumpet lesson.

For a while she rode straight ahead. Chris passed the point where he himself should have turned off to the right, but he decided he could do that later. Grandmother turned left. Chris followed. He stayed as close behind her as he dared. Now they came to a busy intersection with a traffic policeman. The policeman was just raising his hand; everybody had to stop. But no, not everybody; Grandmother was allowed to cross. With a flourish and a friendly nod the policeman let the old lady in the wheelchair through. But Chris had to stop. What a nuisance! No doubt the policeman thought she was a dear old lady going to visit her grandchildren. If only he knew that she was probably on her way to do all sorts of wicked business. But of course you couldn't say that to a policeman. There was nothing Chris could do about the delay. He had to sit there watching as she went on pumping the long handles of her wheelchair and disappeared in the distance.

At last he was able to move again. He pedaled as fast as he could to reduce Grandmother's lead. He had seen her turn off to the left, but he was not sure just where. There were so many side streets here. He looked down each one on the left, but saw no trace of her. Finally he turned left at random. The street was almost certain to be the wrong one, and maybe he was already lost besides. He had never been in this part of the city.

Indecisively he swung off his bike at a bridge over a canal. By chance he glanced along the canal, and then he saw her again. On the next bridge. He had turned left one street too soon.

She was pumping the handles slowly up and down. How strong this old lady was. He knew quite well that the wheelchair certainly didn't go by itself, and that little bridge was very steep.

Now she had reached the top of the arch, and she coasted down the other side rapidly, very rapidly. Chris jumped on his bike at once. This was really exciting. It was quite a distance to the next bridge, and in this neighborhood the street was blocked by barrels, pushcarts, and parked cars. If only she didn't turn off the street before he reached it. He stood up on the pedals so he could see farther, and then he caught sight of the wheelchair. It was not all that far away. Chris rode down the center of the street to skirt an illegally parked car, a taxicab. Chris was about to pass it when it abruptly started off and—Grandmother was gone.

How was that possible? He'd seen her only a minute ago. Amazed, Chris looked around. What a dingy little café. In the window, which was opaque with dirt, hung a sign. The sign showed a picture of a round crocheted doily and bore a notice:

FINE THREAD ASSOCIATION
Needleworkers' Meeting
Thursday, October 5 at 4 P.M.

That was today; that was right now. Could Frank's grandmother have come to this meeting? A needlework club—and for that he was going to be late for his lesson!

But he still could not understand how she could have popped into the café, wheelchair and all. Chris pedaled on a little farther and then walked back. She must be here somewhere. He heard shuffling footsteps. An extremely old, little woman was coming down the street.

She looked even more like a witch than Frank's grandmother, if that were possible, and she turned into a narrow alley alongside the café. Chris watched her. Suddenly she disappeared, but as she did so he saw the wheelchair a short distance beyond her.

Wheeling his bicycle, Chris entered the alley. It was wider than he had thought at first sight. He walked past the wheelchair and then chained and locked his bicycle, planning to go back to see whether he could discover what had become of the old woman. But again he heard someone coming and hid behind the upholstered back of the wheelchair. He saw a young woman with fiery red hair and a long crocheted stole around her shoulders. She was undoubtedly one of the needleworkers. She walked right through the wall of the café. It was very strange. And here was somebody else. This was really interesting, for it was not a woman but the doctor with the bushy eyebrows whom he had seen in Frank's house. Did the doctor spend his spare time crocheting?

After he too disappeared, Chris quietly walked back. There was a door in the wall, an ordinary side entrance to the café. But wasn't it strange that he hadn't seen the door before? And the people who went through it instead of using the glass door at the front of the café were also strange. Suddenly Chris had a wild idea. Of course, that was it. Association of Witches would have attracted too much attention. Fine Thread Association was just a fake name, and you could bet they weren't doing needlework in there. All these weird characters met here to teach each other their tricks or to lend one another books of spells or something like that. He'd thought right off that Grandmother was going to a meeting of witches, and it was so. He certainly wanted to find out more about this.

Chris went back and once more hid behind the wheelchair, for he did not dare go straight through that door. He wanted to take a look around first.

He had hidden just in time. Apparently all the members of the club hadn't arrived yet. A small man with a black, pointed beard and a head sunk between his shoulders came along, and then two fashionably dressed ladies. He would never have thought they would be involved in witchcraft. As quickly and noiselessly as the others, they vanished through the door that you didn't even notice until you went right up to it, so little did it look like a door.

I wish I could see what they're doing, Chris thought. At the end of the alley, extending from the café wall, was a wooden fence, awfully high, but if he climbed on the wheelchair he might be able to hoist himself to the top and peer over it. Nobody had come along for quite a while, and Chris was tired of skulking there in the alley. By now he had clean forgotten about his trumpet lesson.

He climbed onto the wheelchair seat and pulled himself up. Right against the fence, so close that only a cat could slip through between, was a shed. He managed to get up on its roof and cautiously slid forward until he could see something.

He was looking down into an interior courtyard with an old-fashioned pump and moss-grown slabs of stone paving. In the wall that must be the rear wall of the café were a low door and a window with plants on its sill. Some pots of geraniums stood outside. Up against the shed was a wooden scaffold on which stood a few pails and a large watering can. There was a broom leaning against the wall. It was no trick at all to step on the top plank of the scaffold and from there jump to the ground. Chris was in the courtyard. But it seemed he could see nothing of the meeting through the window. He found himself looking into a small kitchen, and he could not very well go in there. Maybe he could climb up on the roof from the shed.

Chris stood quietly looking the shed over. His back was to the little door. A pity that the scaffold isn't closer to the café wall, he thought. The shed roof didn't look any too solid.

"What are you doing here?"

With a start, he turned around. He had heard nothing, but suddenly two people stood there, the red-haired young woman and the doctor. They fixed penetrating stares upon him. The woman had green eyes, and the doctor's eyes had a sinister glitter under those bushy eyebrows. Chris had to think fast.

"I've come for some patterns," he said. "I have an aunt who likes to crochet, and I saw the sign in the window. Can I get crochet patterns for my aunt here?"

How the woman was looking at him! What green eyes. What big eyes. They seemed to be growing. Everything seemed to be growing. The shed all of a sudden looked like a tower. He looked down. His legs were gone; all he could see was a pair of skinny stalks. Something was coming at him, something with long, hard spines. The broom, a broom magnified a hundred times. He could not run away; all he could do was make little hops. He put out his arms to ward off the dangerous thing, but he no longer had arms. He had feathers and he was flying. Chris had become a bird, and he wanted to fly up on the roof of the shed.

He was no longer afraid of the broom because he had already forgotten it. He could still see the figures of the man and woman, but he no longer had any idea what they were. He merely saw brightly colored moving surfaces that frightened him when they began talking to each other, but he could not understand their words. He no longer even knew what he had meant to do in this little courtyard. He did not know himself and had no idea that ever in his life had he bicycled or

hollander

blown a trumpet. Now he was just a small bird hopping along the edge of the roof.

The man and woman were still standing there looking at him.

"What did you turn him into?" the man asked.

"A bird," the woman murmured.

"I thought so."

He looked at Chris, who meanwhile had climbed up to the roof of the shed by way of the scaffold and was there persistently taking little hops with his hands behind his back.

"Dangerous," the man said.

"I thought it was necessary."

"No, you didn't think that. You wanted to show how clever you are. And this little boy is the victim. You should just have directed him to go away."

"But he came here with a purpose. Otherwise he wouldn't have been able to get in. Nobody ever sees this door."

"Just a kid. . . . What purpose would he have?"

"I don't know. Oh, I'm sorry. I shouldn't have done it, but I really thought it was necessary."

"It's dangerous three ways. In the first place he might get hurt, by falling through the roof of the shed or falling off it. He think's he's a bird, but he isn't as light as a bird. In the second place you've done something to his mind. And if he remembers it later, something more will have to be done to his mind. That's against the rules of our association. And in the third place we must get him away from here without his being seen, and if there are people who know that he's in this neighborhood they might come looking for him. That could be very bothersome."

"What should I do?"

"The club will have to decide that. But first of all we must get him off that roof."

The doctor went inside and came back with a piece of bread. He began to scatter crumbs on the ground. Chris jumped down from the shed. He stooped and using his mouth like a beak began pecking up the breadcrumbs from the mossy paving stones. The tall man took hold of him at once and steered him into the shed. There was no lock on the door, but that did not matter. Birds cannot open doors.

Chris sat dazedly on a bench in the park. The twittering of birds in the trees gave him a strong feeling of aversion. He shook his head.

"What's the matter, boy?"

"Are you sick, my boy?"

With an effort, Chris looked up. Two friendly old ladies were bending sympathetically over him.

"What's the matter, boy? Can we help?"

Chris looked at each of them in turn. He had never

seen them before, but still there was something familiar about them. Something about the way they were looking at him prompted him to be on his guard.

"Has something happened to you?"

"No," Chris said, "nothing's happened. How did I get here?"

"Where do you live?"

"On Paradise Street."

"That isn't far. Would you like us to take you home?"

"It must be far," Chris said. "I went farther. . . ."

No, he thought, I mustn't blurt out anything. These are two witches. They look just like Grandmother and the green. . . . There was something green, but what?

He leaned back and closed his eyes. Let them think he was still dazed. He had to remember what they had done to him. He had been biking through the city after Frank's grandmother. Then there was a café. But what happened after that? Ugh, how loudly the birds were chattering. What an annoying racket! What was it that had happened?

The two old ladies stood looking at him very quietly but with deep concern.

"Oh," Chris said, "I think I can find my way home by myself. I feel better now, thank you."

He stood up and started off at a run. The ladies looked somewhat upset as they watched him go. Chris glanced back. If they're witches, he thought, it wouldn't be much of a trick for them to overtake me. But they were not following him, and he slowed his pace. It was in fact not far to his home, and he walked slower and slower. How tired he was.

"Well," his mother said, "good that you're back. Did you find it all right? Chris, what a glassy look you have in your eyes."

"There was a lot of traffic in town," Chris said, "but I had no trouble finding it." That would have been true, too, he thought. At least I was on my way to the trumpet lesson. Oh, and my bike is still standing in that alley!

"You must go to bed early," Mother said, as she watched how listlessly Chris was eating. For the first time in his life he went straight upstairs after supper without protest. First of all he meant to think things over quietly. At the moment his worst worry was what to do about getting his bicycle back. His trumpet was still on the rack, and it was awfully expensive. Despondently he dropped onto his bed. Downstairs the telephone rang.

He began pulling off one shoe. I'll tell her, he thought. As soon as Mother comes upstairs I'll tell her all about it, because otherwise I'm stuck. While he was fussing with his other shoe he heard his mother coming upstairs.

"Are you in bed already? Oh, you've not even finished undressing. Look here, Chris, what did you do this afternoon?"

"I really wanted to tell you about it just now, but it isn't easy because I no longer remember."

"You didn't go to your trumpet lesson. The teacher just called. Where did you go?"

"Maybe I'll be able to find it again. I hope so, because my bike is still parked there."

"Where is your bike?"

"At the café where I was."

"A café! What were you doing there?"

"That's just the trouble. I've forgotten it all. I woke up in the park."

He could sense that his mother was growing angry.

"It really was no fun at all," he said hurriedly. "And it's not over yet." He yawned, happy to have found a good way to put the matter.

"Did you go with anybody?"

"No, nobody at all."

"Then how did you come to be in a café? Chris, now tell me the whole story honestly."

Chris yawned again. A moment ago, when he'd been sitting there alone, he'd wished to tell his mother the whole story, but now he found it much too difficult. She didn't believe in witches. And he was so tired.

"May I tell you tomorrow? I can explain much better after I've slept."

"No, now. You didn't go with anybody. You were on your way to the trumpet lesson. Were you lost?"

"Yes. Yes, that was it. I was lost. I went straight ahead too far. I should have turned right."

"Why did you keep on going straight ahead?"

"There was such a funny vehicle ahead of me. I wanted to know where it was going."

"And then?"

"Well, then I came to the little café, and afterward I don't remember."

"Did you see anybody?"

"Of course. Frank's grandma."

"Frank's grandma?"

"Yes, she was in her wheelchair, of course. But later she disappeared."

"Yes, of course," his mother replied, her face showing no trace of understanding. But she could see how terribly tired Chris was, and at last he had given her a clue she could follow up. She had been afraid of the kind of wicked person who goes after children, but Frank's grandmother. . . . Nobody could be more harmless. She left Chris, and he dropped into a deep sleep. Mother went to the telephone.

Frank's grandmother did not come to the telephone herself, but she readily gave an address. Chris's father drove out there at once to recover the bicycle. He found the café with the sign reading *Fine Thread Association.* Odd, he thought. He found the deserted alley where he saw not a single door or gate. He did not even see the narrow side entrance to the café. But the bicycle was still standing there with the trumpet, safe and sound.

He carried the bicycle to his car and fastened it to the rack. For a moment he stood pensively looking at the café; then he went in. There was no one inside, but a small woman came shuffling in from the rear almost immediately.

Chris's father ordered a glass of beer and remarked, "Not much doing here."

The little woman gestured toward her ear. She was wearing a pink gadget in it with a wire attached, but evidently the hearing aid did not work very well. She could make out what was said to her only when she wanted to.

Chris's father gave one more try. "Are you alone here?"

She was amusingly tiny and looked very cheerful. With a blue rag, she began dusting busily, but she did not say a word. Chris's father finished his beer, paid, and left.

The woman let the coins he had given her drop

tinkling into a drawer, wiped off the table with the blue cloth, and went into the back room, which was crowded with furniture. In front of the window stood an old-fashioned sewing table from which hung a ruffled violet bag trimmed with green chintz. A pair of flowering fuchsias stood on the table.

The woman set the plants on a dresser and lifted the tabletop, which formed a lid. She rummaged around until she had found a skein of fine yarn and a thin crocheting hook. Her hearing was poor, but she could still see everything without glasses. Very swiftly she began crocheting: a small circle, another circle around it, and still another circle in a different stitch. The result looked like a lace collar for a doll.

When it was finished, she put away the yarn and hook, closed the sewing table, and climbed up on a chair. She had two cages hanging in a corner of the room. She opened one of them, releasing a large gray pigeon. The pigeon perched on her hand while she arranged the lace collar around its neck. Then she went outside. In the little courtyard she said to the bird, "Off with you now."

The bird pecked at the collar around its neck, flapped its wings, and soared into the air. It circled twice around the café and disappeared. The tiny woman went back inside and replaced the fuchsias on the table.

While Chris's father was riding home with the bicycle on the luggage rack of his car, the pigeon flew over the city. It knew exactly where it must go: to a big house on a wide street. It came down on a windowsill at the back of the house and tapped against the windowpane with its beak.

The window was opened, and the bird was admitted into the room where three people sat. Two sprightly old ladies were telling about a certain boy in the park, and a dark man was listening. He was frowning so hard that his eyes could no longer be seen.

"Really, Doctor," one old lady was saying, "he didn't know a thing. He said so. He said nothing had happened."

The doctor permitted the pigeon to perch on his hand. With sensitive fingers he removed the collar from its neck and examined the crocheting. He turned the collar around slowly, then handed it to one of his visitors. "I guess he did remember a few things," the doctor said. "Look at this."

The pigeon flew to the back of a chair and began to preen its feathers. The two ladies studied the small crocheted collar carefully.

"Oh, his father has come for the bicycle. I didn't even know there was a bicycle there."

"I didn't know either," the doctor said. "That was a mistake."

"I think," the other woman said, "that nothing of this sort has ever happened before. I really thought we never made mistakes, and now—one oversight after the other. It's so, so unbelievable in our vocation."

The doctor nodded. He took a handful of seed from a cupboard and held it out to the pigeon. After the bird had eaten he opened the window and let it fly away.

"I'm going to call on our sister Southwind," he said. "She knows more about the child."

"I wonder," one of the old ladies said. "Really, I just wonder."

CHAPTER IV

Chris woke up.

"What a crazy dream I've had," he said. "I dreamed I was a bird." It was still very early in the morning and he slept alone in his room, so there was nobody to hear him.

Oh, no, that was yesterday. What a crazy business! He sat up in bed and tried to remember his dream. But the more he pondered it, the vaguer it all became, until in the end he no longer had any idea what he had dreamed. He remembered only that he had left his bike standing in the alley and that later on, in some manner he couldn't understand, he had come to in the park.

Was there time for him to walk into town and recover his bicycle? If it hadn't been stolen in the meantime.

An alarm clock stood beside his bed. It was a quarter to seven. But Chris had no idea how much of a walk it was; he wasn't even sure he could find his way back there, even if the street and all the rest really existed. What was that name again? Fine Thread . . . Society? No, not society, another word, a longer one. He could not recollect. It didn't seem to matter. Should he get out of bed and start walking? See whether all that was real and then come home on his bike?

Or should he try to see whether he could make magic with the stone? He jumped out of bed and took the matchbox from his desk drawer. Then he crawled back under the blankets, for it was cold.

The stone glistened darkly on the cotton. It was very pretty. Chris moved it, and the little white star went bright and dark, bright and dark. It was really terribly careless of Frank's grandma to lose something like this. I'll hang on to it, Chris thought, and keep an eye on it. But he could think of no spell to make, except that his bicycle would come home by itself, for he didn't feel at all like getting out of his warm bed and walking that far. But of course nobody could make that kind of magic.

Chris curled up deliciously and fell asleep again.

Five minutes, and then he awoke with a start. Johanna. He had dreamed that his sister was feeling very bad, that her face was flushed and she was in pain. Chris felt the pain in his head and his throat. This was certainly no dream. Little Johanna. . . .

He got out of bed and ran barefoot to the room across the hall. There was his sister, sitting up in bed, miserable, with tears in her eyes.

"What's the matter?"

There was a hoarse whimper and a whispered, "Mama."

"Are you sick?"

She nodded, and tears overflowed.

"I'll call Mother."

Chris went to knock on Mother's bedroom door.

"Mother, you'd better come. Johanna is sick."

Mother came at once in her slippers and bathrobe. "Chris, you mustn't run around like that; you'll get sick too. What's the matter with Johanna?"

Johanna had a fever and a swollen throat; she could hardly talk and had been unable to call. But after Mother came in and gave her a drink of water, she felt a little better.

Chris stood watching for a while, and then he went to get dressed. It was no longer so early, and he would have to walk to school. It was a long way on foot.

He wrapped the stone in the cotton again and hid it in the same place. This was another miracle. I knew that Johanna was sick, he thought, and I could feel it myself. It's a kind of telescope stone. Now I know for sure that I want to keep it.

Mother was busy warming milk and trimming the crust off the bread for Johanna. By the time Chris finished his breakfast he knew he couldn't make it to school on time.

"Would you write a note?" he said. "Because I'm going to be late."

"No need," Mother said. "You won't be late."

"But I have to walk."

"That won't be necessary. Your bicycle's back. Father brought it."

"He did?" Chris said. "But how did he ever find it?"

"Frank's grandmother told him where it was."

"But—I don't understand."

"I telephoned Frank's mother. But now you'd better get started, or you'll be late after all."

"You shouldn't have done that. I would have been able to find the bike myself. At least I think I would have. And it's terribly, terribly stupid of you to have told Frank's grandmother about this."

"Go along now, Chris."

"All right, but listen. I'm leaving now, but if I have to go home with Frank and if his grandmother does something to me, it'll be a lot of trouble for all of you."

"Then don't go home with Frank."

"All this is over your head," Chris said. "But if you lose me, it won't be my fault. You shouldn't have said anything."

Mother looked anxious as Chris rode off on his bicycle, pedaling vigorously, and she went on looking anxious because Johanna had a very bad cold, and when she telephoned the doctor it turned out that the doctor himself was sick. But what troubled her most were Chris's strange remarks. She could not imagine that Frank's grandmother would want to harm him. She had better have a talk with him after he came back from school.

But just when Chris came home, a doctor for Johanna arrived. Mother was letting the new doctor in at the front door when Chris parked his bike in the shed and clattered into the house. He had the shock of his life, for there was the same man he had seen on the stairs at Frank's house and later at the little café.

"What are you doing here?" Chris demanded.

"Why Chris," Mother said, "say good afternoon nicely. This is Doctor Onkel, who's come to see Johanna."

"He mustn't. You mustn't let him, Mother. Why hasn't Doctor Berg come?"

"Doctor Berg is sick," the man said.

"Did you make him sick? So you could get at my sister? I won't let you. You're not to go upstairs."

"Chris!" Mother exclaimed, appalled.

The doctor laughed, which made him look less sinister. In fact, he seemed rather good-natured. "I don't make anybody sick," he said. "I only make grown-ups and children better. I'm pretty good at that."

"I don't believe you," Chris said.

"Whatever is the matter with you, Chris?" Mother exclaimed.

"It's nothing," Doctor Onkel said. "He's only worried about his sister. But I'd better get right up there and see her."

There was nothing Chris could do; he felt helpless. Morose, he posted himself in front of the window while he listened to the muted sounds from upstairs. In the garden he saw a starling pulling a worm out of the ground. Chris gagged. Was it at the thought of swallowing the worm or because of the matchstick-thin legs under the bird's round body? Maybe I'm getting sick too, just like Johanna, Chris thought. It's not normal for a starling to make me nauseated. And if I get sick that doctor will come to examine me. I don't want him. I'd sooner die. And in a moment Mother will come downstairs again and scold me for being rude to the doctor. I'd better clear out.

Quietly he slipped down the hallway, put on his

jacket, wheeled his bike out of the shed again, and rode off.

But where was he to go? He could ride over to Paul's house and play there, but he really didn't feel like it. I'm stuck again, he thought; it's really awful. Now I have this magic stone and ought to be able to fix things just the way I want them, but instead I'm in trouble. Of course, that's because I still don't know how the thing works. Maybe I'll ride over to Paul's after all. He could come home with me, and we could make magic together.

Paul was busy constructing a ship, the very same one Chris had made.

"I have a ship like that too," Chris said.

"Did you put it together yourself?"

"Of course."

"I'd like to do it all by myself too, but my father keeps butting in."

"Want to come over to my house?"

"I want to finish the ship."

"I have a magic stone at home."

"A what?"

"A magic stone. It really works."

Paul was not impressed. "My cousin had a whole magic box with eggshells and a stick you could lengthen or shorten, and you could make the eggs change color. It was super. What can you do with your stone?"

"I don't really know yet. I want to try it out."

At this Paul looked up with more interest. "Where'd you get it?"

"Found it. Come along now; I have it at home."

"All right. But first I have to hide my ship so my father doesn't mess it up."

Paul began packing all the loose parts into the box and the tube of glue as well. The ship itself was too big for the box now. He placed it on top and carried it carefully up to his room. Chris waited downstairs.

"I hid it in the closet behind my shoes," Paul said.

Together they pedaled over to Paradise Street.

There were all sorts of things Chris's mother wanted to say to him, but with Paul around she couldn't. Chris had been counting on that.

"We're going up to my room to play, and we won't make any mess today."

The first thing Chris did was to take out the matchbox. He lifted the top layer of cotton. "See, this is it."

"Oh," Paul said.

Chris let the light play inside the stone, and Paul saw the star sparkle.

"Neat. Did you find it? And why is it a magic stone?"

"When I hold it tight I sometimes know things that by rights I couldn't possibly know."

Chris told him about the horse in the meadow and

about Johanna's being sick. "But I don't know exactly how it works, because it doesn't work all the time. Suppose you think of something, and I'll hold the stone tight and empty my mind."

"All right."

Chris thought that he was emptying his mind, but that was pretty hard for he saw Paul sitting there and he also saw all the things in his room. Then he closed his eyes and thought, Don't think about Paul and all the things in my room.

"What am I thinking of?" Paul called out.

Chris did not know. "Of a model ship," he said quickly, because that was the first thing that came to his mind.

"Wrong. I thought of your stone."

"Let's try once more. Something different."

"Ready."

"School."

"No, your bicycle bell. Man, that's no magic stone."

"It sure is."

"No way. My cousin's magic kit was just tricks too. Once you know how it's done there's nothing to it, and there really isn't any such thing as magic."

Chris looked unhappy. "There *is* magic. When our teacher acted so crazy he was bewitched. I did that with the stone by accident. I wanted him to become a monkey, and then he thought he was one. I was bewitched once myself, into a bird."

Astonished, Chris looked at the stone in his hand. It had worked again. Now he knew what they had done to him at the café. He thought he had dreamed it, but it had been witchcraft. Now he also remembered the woman's green eyes and understood why watching the starling had made him feel so sickish. It was no fun being a bird. Crazy, really, though it seemed fine to be able to fly.

Paul had turned around and was looking at Chris's model ship, which sat on the low cupboard. He'd had enough of the magic game, since he didn't understand it at all. Chris himself didn't understand why it failed to work sometimes and happened by itself at other times, but he made up his mind to figure it out. With the stone still in his hand he looked at the window and saw two flies chasing each other over the glass. They made him think of a parade with a band playing and everybody walking in step.

In his mind he played a march that he had learned for his trumpet. He was leading a parade, and all the men had to turn left. The flies turned left. Surprised, Chris kept them moving with the gay music: left, right, keeping the beat. He made them walk in a circle, then straight ahead, following one behind the other. Chris was so enthralled that he felt as if he himself were marching with them. It's nice to be a fly, he thought, and then he began to laugh.

"What's up?" Paul asked.

Chris almost said, I've bewitched two flies. But he thought better of it. It was not something he could explain, and he couldn't demonstrate it either, because while he had been busy with the flies he had forgotten Paul's existence. Witchcraft wasn't a matter of thinking or willing something very hard. Rather, you had to feel it, and that was why it was always happening so unexpectedly. Now he'd caught the knack of it anyhow, which put him in wonderfully good humor. He packed away the stone and said, "You're right, it isn't working. Should we play with the cars?"

"Yes," Paul said, "and then we'll build a bridge and make the ship sail under it. You do the cars, and I'll take the ship, OK?"

"OK."

They had lots of fun and gave no more thought to the magic stone. At least Paul did not think any more about it. Chris did. He had made up his mind to practice with it often, but not with Paul or anybody else around. Witchcraft was something you had to do all alone. Later, when he was very good at it, he might show Paul.

Chris stopped hiding the magic stone in the matchbox under absorbent cotton and keeping the box in his desk drawer. Instead he kept the stone in his pocket and felt it now and then. He thought that the more often he cast a spell by accident, the more he would learn about how it worked, until at last he would be able to do whatever he wanted to. He no longer worried about Frank's grandmother, for nothing had happened since that afternoon she had paralyzed him on the stairs, and Mother's telephone call had not stirred up anything.

And soon enough, one morning before school began, he succeeded in carrying off a remarkable piece of witchcraft. Half the children were already in the school playground, and a few of the teachers were also strolling about there. One of the teachers was just arriving on her bicycle. She was well along in years and very strict. Usually she dismounted at the gate and walked her bike stiffly over to the bicycle shed. Chris had seen her do so a hundred times. She was the kind of person he could not imagine ever having been a child. But of course nobody was born grown up. Once upon a time she had probably run fast and ridden her bike without hands, doing fancy turns and figure eights.

And then it happened.

This time she did not dismount but rode her bike right across the playground, very fast, and then she held up both arms and called out, "Look at me, look at me, no hands!"

Everybody looked. She rode around in a circle, her face flushed with excitement, and then one of the other teachers began clapping loudly. All the children cheered. "Hooray. Teacher is riding no hands. Whoopee!"

Everybody had to laugh, of course, and she herself laughed too as she rode up to the bicycle shed and breathlessly dismounted. Two of the bigger boys took the bike and lifted it into the rack for her.

"Terrific, Teach. We never thought you could do it."

Chris enjoyed it all less than the others. He was a bit confused. Now he had done exactly what he had wanted: cast a spell that hurt nobody. But still his success gave him an uncomfortable feeling. The teacher's actions weren't what bothered him, but the knowledge that he and nobody else had made her behave that way. This was the teacher who was always laying down the law, and she was the one he had made bike like a child around the school yard. It was the world turned upside down. And no matter how often Chris might have wished the world to turn upside down, now that it was really happening he no longer thought it was that much fun.

CHAPTER V

Needlework

Frank was not in the habit of telling many stories when he came home from school, but his mother sometimes talked with the other mothers, and so the conversation at the table came around to the odd things that had been happening at school.

"Frank, you're in the same class as Kees and Paul, aren't you?"

"Yes," Frank said.

"Were you there when your teacher got kind of mixed up?"

"Yes, I was there."

"And now another teacher?"

Frank started laughing. "She wasn't mixed up; she was just nice for once. And it's done her a lot of good.

She laughs much more often than she used to. She's a lot better now. She always used to be so stiff."

"I hear from Kees's mother that she biked all over the school yard without hands. That's setting a very bad example."

"Fun," Frank said.

"And just exactly what did happen to your teacher?"

"Oh, he ate a piece of chalk."

"What!"

"He didn't really eat it, because he spit it out again. That was all."

Frank looked at his grandmother. She was listening with keen interest but said nothing.

"The story goes that he acted very strangely," Mother said.

Frank shrugged. What of it? It was great when something different happened in school once in a while. As far as he was concerned all his teachers could act crazy. Fortunately nothing more was said of the matter, but after they were done with dinner and Frank was sprawled out on the rug reading the comic strips in the newspaper, Grandmother said, "I'd be much obliged, Frank, if you would invite that boy once more. That Chris, I mean. Would you ask him whether he'll come to see me sometime?"

"Should it be an invitation, or do I tell him that he has to?"

"No, just make it an invitation. I'd like to talk to him, but if he doesn't want to he doesn't have to. Put it that way."

"All right," Frank said.

Chris received the message the next morning. He did not know what he ought to do. It probably is about the stone, he thought. More than ever he wanted to keep it now, and if he went to see Frank's grandmother he'd probably have to give it back. Of course he could deny knowing about it, but she wouldn't believe him. It would be better not to go, but he was awfully curious and still fearless. It's dangerous, he thought. Maybe she'll bewitch me. I shouldn't go. But then he thought, I'm not scared and I will go.

When he came home for lunch, he went straight upstairs. He deposited his magic stone in the matchbox, wrapped the box in a sheet of newspaper, placed that in a shoe, and shoved it behind his wardrobe.

After school he went along with Frank. In the hallway he grinned and gave the wheelchair a little push. "Should we oil it again?" he asked.

Then he went upstairs and knocked on the door of Grandmother's room. It was a big room, full of plants. There were several bunches of dried flowers strung up. There was a lot of old furniture, little bureaus with many drawers and wobbly tables. He saw books that were not standing side by side in a bookcase but were

piled up on top of each other. And the moment he entered he noticed a pile of magazines. The top one showed an embroidered doily on its cover, just like the one he had seen in the café window. A few of the same kind of doilies lay around on the tables.

"I just wanted to get a good look at you," Grandmother said.

And she looked so long that Chris became jittery. He turned around, saying, "Take a look at the backside too."

She laughed hard at that. "You're a boy of spirit—a boy after my own heart. Tell me this. Have you ever done any needlework?"

"Not me," Chris said.

"I mean knitting or crocheting. Of course boys generally don't do it, but you can learn easily enough. Now listen carefully. Try to find somebody who can teach you needlework, and when you've gotten the hang of how a doily like this is made, come back to see me. Agreed?"

She nodded to him in dismissal.

So that was all. He had to learn needlework. Of all the peculiar things he'd been through lately, this was probably the most peculiar. But Chris didn't brood about it long. He went to play with Frank.

Later, back home, he did start pondering the suggestion. Of course he hadn't any intention of learning needlework. There wasn't even anyone who could teach him, for his mother surely didn't know how. He'd never seen her doing it. Besides, he didn't want to have anything to do with Frank's grandmother. But she had made him curious, and he thought that was pretty crafty of her.

On Sunday Johanna still had to stay in bed. She was transferred to the couch in the living room, and there she lay, bored stiff in the midst of a heap of books, puzzles, magic markers, and other stuff.

"You ought to try doing a little needlework," Chris suggested.

Mother began to laugh. "What made you think of that?"

"Oh," Chris said, "I think she might find it fun."

"You're right, Chris," Mother said. "I couldn't help laughing because you sounded so condescending, but it's really an excellent idea. When I was small and had the measles, my mother taught me to crochet, and now I'll teach Johanna."

"Do you know how?" Chris asked incredulously. "You never do it."

"Let's see whether I still know how," Mother said.

First all the other stuff was cleared off the couch, and then Mother hunted up yarn and crochet hooks. Chris stood by, watching it all closely.

"You can't do it," Johanna said. "You're a boy."

"I can too," Chris said. "Just let me get the hang of it, and you'll see that being a boy has nothing to do with it."

"That's right, you'll see," Mother said, and Chris was given a crochet hook.

First they learned the slack and taut and long stitches. These were fairly easy, although you had to be careful about getting the edges straight. Chris now wanted to know how you could make a round doily, and Mother even knew that, but she had forgotten the stitches for making most other things.

When Father came home, they were all three sitting and crocheting.

"Well, what a sight," Father said. "Now you can all three become members of that association."

"What do you mean?"

"The Fine Thread Association. That was the name in the window of Chris's café."

"Oh, come on," Chris said angrily. "I wouldn't want to be in with that crowd. I just want to know how it's done."

"Very sensible. You never know when a skill like that may come in handy. Now at least you can make your living by crocheting potholders."

Chris dismissed the remark airily. "Someday I'm going to be rich," he said.

* * *

Doctor Onkel went by bicycle from one patient to the next. He had fewer patients than most doctors, and he usually stayed longer with each. One of his patients was Frank's grandmother.

She was not sick. When he entered her room he found her looking livelier than ever. The doctor gave her a grave look. "How are you feeling today, Sister Southwind?"

"Very well," Grandmother said. "Very well indeed, Brother Onkel."

"Some people are worried."

"Don't let it bother you. Some people always worry."

"They are the people of our association. A stitch has dropped out of the fabric. Do you know any more about that, Sister Southwind?"

She chuckled. "I'm not worried about it, Brother Onkel."

"You are one of our oldest members and have committed the most follies."

"I like follies. Besides, mine have always turned out well."

"Ten years ago when you tried to fly off the roof on a broomstick you took a bad fall."

"There wasn't room enough for a landing, but otherwise the experiment was successful. I did it because I didn't want one of our oldest arts to be lost."

"At the moment one of our greatest treasures is in

the hands of a small boy. That is not just foolish; it's dangerous."

"As far as I can see he's handling the matter very sensibly. You've all kept after me for years about choosing a successor. So that's what I'm doing. Let me take care of it my way."

"Sister Southwind, you have a daughter and a granddaughter."

"They're not suitable, and this boy is."

"Was it essential to entrust the stone to him so soon?"

"No, that happened by accident, but mightn't it be wise to make good use of an accident?"

"Our web extends over the whole world. Wherever the threads are stretched, there is somebody holding them taut. Every man in power has someone near him, a wife or a woman friend or some other aide who knows what is in his mind and who wisely guides him to the right decisions. The web is wide and the thread is thin, and the fate of the world hangs by that thread."

"You certainly don't have to tell me all that."

"What else can I say? What can I do to change your mind?"

"But my dear man, the moment you came in I could read in your face everything you were going to say. There's no way you can make me change my mind. You must realize that."

The doctor sighed. He did realize it. But he had hoped she would listen to him. This was the way it always was. With his patients, too. He knew what was the matter with them and what they had to do to get better, but there were all too many who really wanted to stay sick. And this old lady—you really couldn't call her sick, but she was stubborn, dreadfully stubborn. She should have begun long ago to initiate someone gradually into the secrets of the association, but she'd always made excuses. Nobody was just right. And now all of a sudden a child was playing with the stone. In the whole world there were only a few objects that had such great power. Everyone in the association hoped to have the stone after her. But unreasonable as she was, she went and gave it to a mere boy. Or even worse, didn't give it. "An accident," she had said. Maybe she didn't even know how the stone had come into his possession.

"Very impressive," she said. "You certainly know how to frown with those eyebrows of yours. At our last meeting I was quite disgusted by all the talk of gloom and doom. When I heard that a boy had tried to crash the meeting, I thought, Ha! Later his mother telephoned and it proved to be my boy, and I again thought, Ha! Do you know what he has been up to? Made one of the teachers do tricks so that the whole school laughed, and she laughed right along. To my mind that shows talent, although my daughter says it's a bad example. You see why she would never do. Always worrying. I don't worry. I consider worrying a bad character trait."

"I shall have to report on this to the membership," Doctor Onkel said.

"Go right ahead. It doesn't worry me."

The doctor left, and Grandmother began rummaging through one of her bureaus. She pulled out one drawer after the other, mumbling to herself all the while. "Let him go ahead. Let them all go ahead. They won't get the better of me. I'm the oldest here, and I know whom to turn to. Where in the world did I put it?" She looked in another bureau. "I couldn't have known that either —that I'd need her again sometime. Ha-ha-ha, what a surprise it will be for her! What fun we used to have together! Where in the world is it? All these idiots here are just waiting to latch on to my stone, but I'll show them. Ah, here it is."

Triumphant, she brought out a thin, tattered doily. It was a bit dirty, too, but she laid it on the table as if it were something very precious. After she had studied it long and carefully, she took a small ball of yarn and a crochet hook from her sewing box, sat back in an easy chair, and hooked rapidly away. She worked so fast that she made a mistake.

Annoyed, she unraveled her work. "Don't rush so,"

she cautioned herself. "We'll get nowhere this way."

She began again, somewhat more deliberately. She crocheted a small, round doily with a very curious pattern.

Meanwhile, the doctor in his wide cape was bicycling down the streets. He came to a busy avenue and followed it for a long stretch. Then he turned left and crossed a small bridge. At last he arrived at the dingy old café. He went straight in, and the small, bright-faced woman showed him into the back room.

"Would you run up something for me, Fleurtje? I haven't the time to do it myself."

Fleurtje moved the houseplant that occupied the middle of a table and brought out a large book with ancient, yellowed pages. It was full of patterns and stitches. The doctor obviously understood them and knew his way about the book. He found the pages he wanted and showed her exactly what he had in mind. She nodded and brought him some tea in a small, round pot.

After he had drunk a cup of fragrant tea, Doctor Onkel mounted his bicycle again and went calling on more patients. Little Fleurtje replaced the houseplant, flanking it with the two fuchsias that had been on the windowsill. She opened her sewing table and took out the things she needed. Quickly and skillfully she began to crochet.

And back home on Paradise Street Chris also crocheted. Not quickly and not at all skillfully, but still he made more progress than Johanna.

"Look at my doily! I'm way ahead of you!"

"It's silly for a boy to crochet, isn't it, Mama?"

"What's silly about it?"

"I don't want Chris to do it better than me. Look, he's way ahead."

"He goes a bit faster than you, but that's because your hands are smaller. Your work is very pretty."

"My stitches are pretty, Chris."

Chris looked curiously at Johanna's work. Was it really prettier than his, or was Mother just saying that to soothe her feelings? Should he quickly reach for his stone and make a spell so that Johanna's crocheting would get all snarled up? He saw what a hard time she had drawing the thread through the loop. Yes, her hands were really awfully small. He would not get her work snarled.

I had really better watch my step, Chris suddenly thought. I wouldn't want to become a wicked witch like Frank's grandma. It's true I'm learning how to crochet, but I'm not doing it because she said so. Maybe she did put the idea into my head, but I'll keep out of her way from now on.

Chris had no idea what plan Frank's grandmother was nursing. But before long quite a number of people would be finding out. In a few days all the members of the Fine Thread Association would receive a sheet of paper showing the pattern of the doily that Fleurtje was at this moment crocheting.

CHAPTER VI

The Cat Woman

A smooth little object like a magic stone is easily lost, but Chris wanted to have it with him all the time. Therefore, he kept it safely packed in the matchbox and the box in his pocket. He had it with him when he went to school, when he played soccer, and even when he went to his trumpet lesson. He took the streetcar now because he was no longer allowed to bike into town. Mother was afraid he would get lost. She exaggerated terribly, of course.

One day in the streetcar he saw a woman wearing a long openwork wool stole. Now that he could crochet, Chris could see how the stole had been made. I could do it too, he thought; I could make a stole as good as that, but I wouldn't know who there'd be to wear it. It wouldn't be right for Mother, which was a pity; it looked so beautiful, and the woman's long red hair was beautiful, too.

He had seen her before. And suddenly Chris was forcibly reminded of the day he had been bewitched, of that horrible feeling of being a bird without hands, a ball of feathers on matchstick legs without understanding of the things around him. He knew that this woman was the one who had done that to him, and he felt such a rage growing in him that he would have liked to bash her with his trumpet case, but he thought better of it just in time. Instead he put down the case and reached for the matchbox in his pocket. He opened it and fumbled in the cotton. Then he gripped the stone tightly in his hand and felt strong and mighty.

The woman turned around and looked at him. Chris had completely forgotten how burning her green eyes were. She was a cat. And suddenly he saw her as nothing but a cat with a big paw full of curving claws reaching out toward his hand that held the stone.

That confused him. He had wanted to cast a spell on her, but hadn't figured out how to go about it. And he did not yet know that people like her could sense when someone was angry at them. She had attacked him before he could defend himself. Now she probably wanted him to think again that he was a poor little bird. But by now Chris had gathered some experience in magic. He knew that those razor-sharp claws on that monstrously big cat's paw were not real. She wanted to get hold of his stone—that was what he sensed—but she wouldn't get it away from him. I'll take care of you, Chris thought, you sly red cat. You are a cat; you're really a cat. You want me to think so, but I want you to believe it yourself.

The people on the streetcar did not see that a silent battle was going on between the boy with the trumpet case and the red-haired woman, but a few people looked up in astonishment when they suddenly heard a clear "meow-r-r-r."

Chris realized that his spell had worked. He sighed with relief and looked around. Oh, he had to get off; he'd already gone one stop too far. Quickly he grabbed his case and jumped off the streetcar. Not for a moment did he consider that he was leaving behind someone who thought she was a cat.

The incident had upset him and left him shaking—all the more since he had to run fast to make his music lesson in time. And he played badly.

"You had better improve your tone," his teacher said. "That sounds like caterwauling."

"No wonder," Chris said. "On the way here I was frightened by a cat."

"How could a cat frighten you? I hope you weren't mistreating it."

"Oh, I sure was," Chris said with satisfaction.

The teacher gave him a sharp look. Was this the kind of boy who mistreated animals? He never would have thought Chris capable of that sort of thing. Oh well, it was none of his affair. His job was to teach the child to play the trumpet; the rest was his parents' responsibility.

Together they struggled through the lesson. They'd never had one that dragged on so hopelessly.

Next day there was a story in the newspaper that a streetcar conductor had had his face scratched by a woman who did not want to get off. She tried to scratch everybody who came close to her and could not speak, could only make mewing sounds. A doctor had calmed her down. She turned out to be a well-known painter, who sometimes suffered from mental derangement.

When Frank's grandmother came across this little item, she first started cleaning her glasses, then read the story once more. "Well-known painter," she mumbled to herself. "That was certainly Selina. And my boy Chris bewitched her with the stone. Only my stone is powerful enough for that. Scratched the conductor's face . . . mental derangement . . . ha-ha-ha! Fit to be tied she must be. I think I'll have to do something now. There's going to be real trouble, and he won't be able to cope with it. I'll have to swoop him out of the way for a while. Maybe she'll get the whole association into action. What fun. It's a long time since I've had something to do."

She let her glasses slide down her nose and sat in thought for a while. Every now and then she chortled to herself, and her dark eyes glowed with delight. After some fifteen minutes she hobbled down the stairs. Her daughter was in the kitchen, washing dishes. Grandmother sat down on a low stool near her.

"Listen," she said, "I feel the need for a change of air. What if I rented a house in the woods, one of those little vacation houses you can rent by the week? With the fall vacation coming up, I could take Frank and that friend of his along. I'd like to be in country where lots of mushrooms grow. City children lose touch with nature. It would be nice for them to learn something about mushrooms." She nodded contentedly. This last point had just occurred to her.

"But Mother, how will you manage? Cooking, making the beds. . . ."

"The boys will help me. All that will be educational for them."

"It strikes me as an odd and unreasonable plan. I can't imagine what Chris's parents will say to it."

"Don't let that worry you. You know that when I make up my mind about something I have it my way. All I'm asking you is to get hold of cottage listings and check the schedules to see when the trains are. Will you take care of that?"

"I'll do it this afternoon, Mother."

"Then that's settled."

Grandmother stood up with an effort. Bracing herself on the counter, she hobbled out of the kitchen. She was a long time getting back to her room. And when she did, she gave a sigh. A pity that she walked so poorly. She was just about to settle into her easy chair when she heard a tapping against the windowpane. On the windowsill sat a large crow.

Selina the cat woman lived in an attic with a huge skylight. She was famous for her drawings of birds. Selina had only to scatter bread and seed, and birds came flocking into her room. She had the power to make them sit still for hours, so that she had time to draw them with great precision. The people she painted also sat still for hours. When they sat for her, they lost all sense of time until their portraits were finished, and then they said, "Is that me? I didn't know I was like that, but now I see it. It's true. That's the way I am." From that moment on they knew themselves better.

Two men were visiting Selina, both members of the association. One was Doctor Onkel, who had brought her back to her senses in the streetcar. The other was Tony, whom everybody called Toontje. He was a cobbler by trade, a small person with hunched shoulders and a pointed beard. Toontje had read the newspaper account and had come at once, for he was one of the artist Selina's admirers. He himself was a grand story-teller. He told stories you never forgot, and jokes that could send you off into gales of laughter an hour later. The doctor thought highly of him.

All three of them had agreed that the stone must not be left in a boy's hands. Something had to be done. But what?

"We must not get it from him by trickery," the doctor said. "The association forbids all falsehoods, especially toward a child. We must make him understand that it is wrong for him to possess an object of such power. He must give it up of his own accord."

"He never will. I tried to scare him, but he turned the tables on me, the little monster."

"But surely he ought to see for himself that it's necessary."

"All human beings do things that are wrong. Why? Because they enjoy it. Can you think of a plaything that is more fun than an authentic magic stone?"

"We must show him the truth, and then he will believe us."

"Our truth."

"Of course, our truth. Even with his stone he could never overcome the three of us."

"Sister Southwind has different ideas about the truth."

"She is old and no longer sees the real truth."

"Then let us discuss precisely what that truth is."

"The magic stone in the hands of a child is a danger to the world."

"Yes, that is so. The magic stone in the hands of a child is a danger to the world. And how are we going to make him realize that? By all of us coming down on him together?"

"No, certainly not. We don't want him to think that we are after the stone for ourselves. He must believe that he has decided to get rid of it. And Toontje is the man who must talk to him. He already knows the two of us, but he has never seen Toontje. Besides, neither of us is as good with children as Toontje."

"Exactly," the cobbler said. "The magic stone in the hands of a child, and so on. I'll bombard him with all that. And then? What is he supposed to do with the stone? Take it back to Sister Southwind? Or am I to take it into my charge?"

The tone of the conference chilled. It was as if the shadow of a black cloud had suddenly fallen over a sunny landscape. Suddenly all three of them realized that the truth was something bigger than each one's notion of it. They did not want Chris to have the stone, nor should it go back to Sister Southwind, because she had handled it carelessly. They wanted it themselves. Each of them wanted it, but so did all the others in the city who knew of its existence, and even witches and sorcerers from distant cities and countries would very much like to have that magical little thing. Who was going to get it?

Selina was the first to break the silence. "We are greedy. That's it. And I thought I had got over that long ago. Oh, I wish that stone didn't exist."

Doctor Onkel said, "We must each give it up in advance."

"We can bring the question to the meeting and let the association decide."

"We're talking as though we already had it," Toontje said. "Let's not get ahead of ourselves. I was only asking."

Selina stood up. "Let us have something to drink. I'll make a tea that clears head and heart. You know, I really do my best to be clearheaded, but it's often very hard."

She dropped a few sticks of wood into a small, round stove, and soon the kettle began to sing. She went over to a round cupboard in the corner that stood on curved legs. There were tiny drawers even in the legs. From the top drawer and from the sixth from the top, she took some herbs and sprinkled them into the steaming kettle. No one spoke while the fragrant steam filled the room. Then Selina poured the tea into a blue bowl, and each of them sipped from it in turn. This was real witchcraft.

In the rain gutter outside the window sat a large crow. It peered through the windowpane with intelligent eyes.

When the blue bowl was empty, the men stood up and left without saying a word. That was the way things were done.

The little cobbler trudged off to the small basement shop where he worked. As he wended his way through narrow streets he grinned as he thought over what he might tell Chris.

The doctor rode off on his bicycle with a troubled face showing above his wide, flapping cape. I must stay nearby, he thought. I have to keep an eye on the boy in case something happens.

After the men had left, Selina opened the window. She let in the crow but did not begin sketching it. She had something else in mind.

Crows are partial to glittering objects, she thought, and birds can get to many places. It would be nice if the crow could steal the stone and bring it here to me.

The crow perched on the arm of the chair, as she wished, and she looked fixedly at it. It blinked its eyes and boldly returned her look. She had never seen a bird

that could stare in such a human way. Now that she had its attention she turned her thoughts to the stone and the boy, picturing to herself the neighborhood where he lived and where he went to school. The crow would have to locate him. It shifted back and forth on the arm of the chair, rather frightened by her glittering green eyes.

Then it flew off before Selina thought she had finished with it. It flapped its wings and soared out through the window. Its caw-caw-caw sounded like the hoarse laughter of an old man.

Chris sat in his room. The stone lay on the desk in front of him. He wanted to use it to make magic, but he wasn't able to. He could not concentrate his thoughts. He kept thinking about people and things he did not want to think about at all. It was tiring, and he became a bit irritable. He could not understand why this was happening.

Why was it he kept seeing the cat woman? Sometimes she appeared in a blue vapor, another time covered with black feathers. And he saw Doctor Onkel bicycling rapidly past the school, his cape billowing behind him like the sail of a ship. Go away, Chris thought. I know for sure he's a fraud. And there was Frank's grandmother, sitting on a bench and shaking with laughter, while a landscape of houses and trees flew by. These visions felt like memories, but he had never seen any of these people in such situations.

And then there was someone else whom he thought he knew, but he couldn't place him. A short man with a pointed beard. He was behaving even more strangely than the others. A castle sprang up from the ground, with great bramble bushes all around it. The man waved his arms and the castle and everything else disappeared, but in its place was a deep hole. Plop, something fell into it. The stone! Chris knew it was the stone and that the man was waiting deep inside the pit. He opened his mouth and swallowed the stone.

Suddenly Chris knew where he had seen this man: in the vicinity of the café while he himself was hiding behind Grandmother's wheelchair. All these people had something to do with witchcraft. And then Chris realized that the stone was making him think of them. It was like the time Johanna had been sick. But that time it had been something real, while all these things he was seeing meant nothing.

But as soon as Chris stopped fighting against his thoughts, everything became a good deal clearer. The blue steam was coming from a bowl that three individuals were drinking out of. He knew they were thinking about him, and he did not like that. Then he thought of Frank's grandmother. She was sitting in a bus, or something like it, and he himself was sitting next to her. To his surprise, he had a pleasant feeling. That ought not to be so. Witchcraft was bad; therefore Grandmother was bad also. He didn't want to have anything to do with it or her.

Chris put the stone away in his drawer and went out to play. When he returned, his mother said, "I have a surprise for you."

"What is it?"

"Frank is going away for fall vacation and wants you to come along."

"He does? Where to?"

"To a forest somewhere. You'd enjoy that, wouldn't you? When we went away, you were bound and determined to stay with Frank. So I guess he is your best friend."

"Oh, sure. I like the idea. A forest sounds super to me."

"Frank's grandmother is taking a little house there, just for the three of you."

"Oh, no, I don't want to go with that grandmother. She's a bad sort. I told you that before."

"Oh, Chris, what nonsense!"

"I won't go."

"All right, I'll tell them no, though it seems a pity."

CHAPTER VII

The Stone Ghost

Grandmother was offended. She had had her daughter telephone, and Chris's mother had said, "How lovely! I'm sure he'll be delighted to go." And half an hour later he did not want to come. Such a stupid boy. If only he had some idea of what was hanging over his head. Grandmother herself did not know the whole story, but she had inklings. The doctor and Selina wanted to get hold of the stone, and goodness knows how many others besides. All the members of the Fine Thread Association had found in their mailboxes the pattern that told them Chris had the magic stone. Grandmother was well aware of how envious they had been of her, particularly in the past, when she had been able to get about easily and used to take care of everything so efficiently. In recent years, of course, they had hoped she would die without a successor. But no, she was far from dead yet, and she had a successor, whether or not he wanted the job. And he would come with her, too. Another new doily was already on its way to her old friend. They were expected there in a few days, so there was nothing for them to do but go.

Next morning Grandmother announced that she had to go into town. Before he left for school Frank had brought her satchel down to the hall for her. His mother had to bump the wheelchair over the threshold. Grandmother tucked her two canes into a holder at the back of the chair, and then off she went, as ready for battle as an old soldier.

Selina set out at about the same time. She had stayed in her attic all day long, looking for the crow to appear. Her window gave her a view of an ocean of roofs with tall chimneys and old rain gutters on which birds perched to take a rest from flying. Selina knew many of the birds individually, and all the pigeons, starlings, sparrows, and titmice that had ever been to her studio knew how to find the skylight where the food was scattered every day.

A thousand other birds peered inquisitively in through the glass while she waited for that one crow.

All day long she paced restlessly back and forth, wondering whether the crow might have got hurt after it had successfully stolen the stone.

By the next morning she could stand it no longer. She went to the neighborhood where Chris lived, where the doctor was bicycling around whenever he had the time, and where the cobbler was also on the lookout, since he had at last thought up a good story. Not one about bears or castles, and not about a pit either. None of those was good enough. No, he was going to tell about ghosts, real spooks in white sheets. In fact, he had brought a sheet with him, plastic, so it folded up small as a handkerchief and could be tucked into the inside pocket of his overcoat. Beaming with delight, the cobbler stationed himself near the school where Chris should be coming out. But he did not know him. He had to ask someone who Chris was. Maybe that girl with the jump rope would tell him.

"Hello, young lady, can you tell me which of the boys is Chris?"

"He isn't here," the girl replied. "He had to stay in."

Chris had to finish an arithmetic example and was sitting alone in the classroom. When he was fairly close to finishing up an example, he could always manage to speed through the last steps and get it done in the allotted time. But when he realized that time was running out and he was still far from finishing, he found he could not work on it at all. He was in that fix now and was just sitting and gazing out the window.

And then the ghost appeared. First it hung in a tree like washing from the line, but then it came closer, and Chris could see that it had eyes, pitiful old eyes, although the ghost was as small as a three-year-old child. It fluttered back and forth in front of the open window and then came in. Flabbergasted, Chris watched as it floated across the classroom and stopped in front of the blackboard.

A real ghost, he thought. By all rights I should be afraid of it, but it strikes me as only pitiful.

There was a vigorous rapping on the windowpane. A bearded man stood outside, gesturing. Hesitantly Chris went over to the window.

It was the same man, the man from the café, who had drunk from the bowl with the cat woman. And of course it was a fake ghost. When were those witches and sorcerers going to stop badgering him?

"Grab him," the man shouted, "grab him, or if you're afraid to, let me in so I can grab him."

"Why?" Chris asked. "He's not doing any harm."

But the man was already climbing in through the window. In a few strides he reached the blackboard to which the white thing was clinging. He seized it, folded it, and tucked it into an inside pocket of his overcoat.

"He does no harm, but he always wants to roam. This is a stone ghost, and that kind are never at rest. Again and again he manages to escape, and then he starts roaming around at once. That will go on forever. They are pitiable creatures, these stone ghosts. You see, they're diluted."

"Oh?" Chris said.

The man sat down on a desk and let his legs dangle, but he kept his hand pressed firmly against the pocket.

"Once upon a time he was an ordinary human being, but then one way or another he got hold of a magic stone. A witch can make magic with one of those things; she has the power. But when an ordinary person does so, it seems to work nicely at first, but his strength wears out because he doesn't have the witch's power. After a while he gets to be just like this poor little ghost. He can't eat or sleep anymore, can't do anything but roam. Sad, isn't it?"

"Yes," Chris said.

"Have you ever seen a ghost like that before?"

"No, never."

"I just wonder why he came in here. Why are you staying after school, anyhow?"

Chris looked unhappily down at his paper. Come to think of it, he had to do that example.

"Ha-ha," the man said. "You having trouble with

your arithmetic? Let me help you. One good turn deserves another. I'm good at figuring because I'm a cobbler. I have to know what to charge people for having their shoes mended. What do you want to be when you grow up, or haven't you decided?"

"I'm going to be rich," Chris said.

"Good idea, ha-ha."

The man hopped off the desk and slid into the seat next to Chris. He reached for Chris's paper and began writing down numerals quickly. They looked just as if Chris had written them himself.

"There, how do you like that?"

The man grinned cheerfully at him, his eyes so screwed up with laughter they were almost closed. He had the face of a jolly elf rather than a wicked sorcerer.

"Why did you pull that trick?" Chris asked. "I mean, that trick with the ghost."

The man looked thoughtfully at him, his hand stroking his beard.

"You see, I don't believe a word of it," Chris said.

"Why did I do it? The magic stone in the hands of a child is a danger to the world. That's why. I have to make you realize that. But that's something I could do by just discussing the matter with you—maybe better. So it's a good thing you asked me. Now we can talk about it."

While the man spoke, Chris got up and went to the

door with his arithmetic paper. Once in the hall, he ran as fast as he could toward the room where the teacher was. He was supervising some other kids who were staying in for a variety of reasons. Chris lingered there as long as he could, because he did not want to meet the cobbler again. He hoped the man would leave as he had come, through the window. Slowly Chris walked down the deserted hall. Once outside, he kept looking around cautiously. His bicycle stood alone in the shed.

Several sparrows flew up. How strange the school yard looked when no one was around. The front of the bicycle shed was open; its back wall ran along the street. It was roofed with corrugated iron. Just as Chris was about to take his bicycle, he heard voices in the street, excited voices. Someone was saying, "I don't know, I don't know, I don't know."

He recognized the voice of the cobbler. Chris replaced his bike in the rack. He hoisted himself up on the corrugated roof from where he could see what was happening out in the street. Lying on his belly, he saw a remarkable group of people. The cobbler was there, the cat woman, and two finely dressed young ladies with big fur collars and long silk-stockinged legs. And then there was the doctor, looking dignified, standing at least a head taller than the others.

"You want the magic stone," the cat woman said accusingly to the two glamorous young ladies.

"Of course we do. Why should you want it and we not."

"Sisters," the doctor said, "brothers and sisters, let us be reasonable."

"Oh, look," Selina exclaimed.

Grandmother came rolling around the corner in her wheelchair.

"Greetings, brothers and sisters," she called out cheerily. "What a lucky chance, meeting you here. Greetings, Chris, nice that you're here too."

Chris quickly drew his head back, but the doctor had already spied him. "Don't run away, boy. We are friends."

Tell me another, Chris thought. He slid down the roof, grabbed his bike, and tore across the school yard. Luckily, the gate was on the other side of the yard. He did not have to pass through the street where the sorcerers were gathered.

But they did not stand still. The cobbler vaulted the fence by the bicycle shed and ran after him. The doctor jumped on his own bicycle and circled the school. Grandmother started her wheelchair off in the other direction. With powerful pulls she worked the two handles up and down, and she moved almost as fast as Chris and Frank had when they rode in the wheelchair together. The two ladies jumped into their sports car and followed her.

Selina was left alone. She had no car and no bicycle, and she saw no point in climbing the fence. There was in fact no point. The cobbler was a fast runner, but he did not catch up to Chris. Pleased with himself, Chris looked around triumphantly as he sped down the street. Then he looked to the right and saw that Grandmother was catching up to him, and the car was behind her. He looked to the left, and there was Doctor Onkel, perilously close. Chris swerved to the left, where he anticipated the least danger. But the doctor stretched out a long arm and seized him. He had to dismount.

"Let go of me."

"I'm here to help you. These women are totally unpredictable. I don't want anything to happen to you. It's an extremely unpleasant situation, but I'll take you safely home."

"I can get home by myself," Chris protested, but the doctor had already pulled him onto the handlebars of his bicycle.

"My bike. I don't want to, I don't want to. Help, police, help!"

There was no policeman in the vicinity, and the teacher, who was still in the school, did not come out.

In spite of his resistance Chris was being carried off.

But at this moment Grandmother came riding up at full speed. She caught up with the doctor, who was weaving as he tried to keep the bicycle moving while hanging on to a struggling Chris.

"I'll help you," Grandmother cried. "Watch out now. You're going to fall."

Grasping one of her canes by its tip, she hooked the handle around the front wheel of Doctor Onkel's bicycle. The two riders tumbled to the pavement. Chris was on his feet in a moment, with only one thought: escape. But where? The cobbler had already seized his bicycle. The two ladies had meanwhile got out of their car. One of them was bending over the doctor, who was sitting on the ground rubbing his head, while the other, flashing a great smile, was bearing down on Chris. Grandmother had been going along at such a clip that she rode on past, but now she swung around and came toward him. And Selina was sauntering in their direction from the other end of the street.

"Come here, boy," Grandmother ordered.

She still had the cane in her hand, and she pounded it against the little footboard of her wheelchair.

"Stand right here."

She shifted somewhat to one side, and Chris stepped on the board. Like that time on Frank's stairs when Chris had been unable to move, he had to do what she wanted, but now he did not find the sensation unpleasant.

"I'm tougher than the whole lot of them," Grandmother said contentedly.

She rode off with Chris as a passenger. She was not going so very fast, but nobody pursued them. Even Selina did nothing to stop them. As they rode past her, Chris heard a hoarse laugh like that of an old man. It came from a big crow that fluttered wildly around her. A moment later it came down on Grandmother's cane, which was again stowed away with the other one in the holder at the back of the wheelchair. The crow rode along, perched on the handle of the cane. Selina watched with her green cat's eyes.

"You might cooperate with me on this."

Chris took one of the handles, and Grandmother began working the other with two hands. Their speed increased.

"Now do you see why I was arranging to have you go to the forest with me? It's better to clear out of here for a while, because what just happened is only the beginning. It will get worse and worse. There are a lot more of them, and they're all after your stone. I have to teach you how to handle it. Otherwise, you'll never be able to defend yourself. Where do you have it, anyway?"

"At home."

"You should have said that right off. I thought you always kept it on you. Now we'll have to go and get it first. I was on the way to the station."

They had come into a busier part of town. At a stoplight Grandmother turned the wheelchair and rode back the way they had come. Many people stared in astonishment at the peculiar group. The crow was still perched behind them. Chris stood rather uncomfortably on the narrow footboard. He was getting tired, and he wondered at Grandmother's strength. Keeping up this pace didn't make her turn a hair. A witch's power evidently. How much of the cobbler's story was true?

Alarmed, Chris realized what was afoot. They had already been on their way to the station, and he still did not want to go along to that cottage in the forest. Anyhow he had to go to school tomorrow; the fall vacation would not begin until next week. And his bicycle was still lying there on the street, or else someone had taken it and he would never get it back. If he went along with Frank's grandmother, maybe he himself would never come back home. At first he had enjoyed seeing all those people standing there dumbfounded. Now he was no longer enjoying the adventure. But fortunately they were on the way home. No point jumping off, because the wheelchair was going as fast as he could.

"You'll pack your toothbrush," Grandmother was saying, "and I guess you can write a note for your mother. But don't dawdle."

Mother will probably be home, Chris thought. Should I say that I'm practically being kidnapped? In any case, I'll make it clear that I don't want to go.

But Mother was not home. Nobody was home. He had to go up and fetch the stone and his toothbrush; there seemed no way out of it. Grandmother stayed in her wheelchair. Chris took the box out of the drawer and looked down at Grandmother through the window. How old she was and thin as a sheet of paper.

He opened the box, and when he had the stone in his hand he saw her differently, no longer so frail, rather strong and rather fierce. He would never be able to bewitch her. He would not even want to, because in spite of everything she could not be different from what she was. This Chris now knew. But after all, that was true of everyone. I don't want to bewitch anyone, he thought. She can have her stone back. Resolutely he went down the stairs and out the front door.

"I'm not going with you."

"Of course you're going."

"I don't want to, and I don't want the stone either. Here, please take it."

"Why don't you want the stone?" She did not take it.

"It's bad. At first I thought it was fun to have it, but now I think otherwise. It's bad."

"That depends on who has it. Are you of the opinion that you know already what things are bad?"

"Yes."

"Well, so you do, and that's why you are the right person to be my successor. The stone is a window into a wider world and—but let's go. Hop on. I'm going to teach you all that."

"I don't want to."

Chris stared at the footboard. Something in him longed to step up on it and speed along into that wider world. But he did not move.

"What do you want?"

"I want to be rich when I grow up, and then I can do what I want. I'll buy myself a house in a forest."

"The world shrinks more and more for people who are rich and can do what they want. Can you conceive of anything more stupid than that?"

Grandmother tried to look into his eyes, but Chris just stood there staring obstinately at the footboard. Abruptly Grandmother started up the wheelchair and rolled away.

"Here's the stone," Chris shouted after her. "The magic stone. I don't want to keep it."

She paid no attention, and Chris angrily threw the

stone after her. It fell to the pavement, and at once the crow came flying down out of a tree. It was the same crow that had perched on the cane for so long and that had stayed close to them, watching whatever happened. With a cackling laugh it swooped to the ground, picked up the stone, and flew off with wings flapping powerfully.

Chris went inside, feeling very sad. Now he was rid of his stone, and he was going to miss it badly. He had also caused an old woman grief.

"Horrid old witch," he murmured. But he did not mean it. He knew that he was already rather fond of Grandmother and that he would be fonder of her the more he got to know her. That was a depressing thought.

"Horrid witch," he said again.

He noticed a ball of yarn. There lay the needlework. He felt the need of something to keep his fingers busy, and so he began to crochet.

CHAPTER VIII

Chris Must Decamp

Crocheting once around is called a row. Chris did two rows. Then he recalled that Grandmother was the one who had advised him to learn crocheting. Why had she done that? Could you cast spells by crocheting? For safety's sake he put the needlework away. Then the doorbell rang.

Slowly Chris went to the front door. What a nuisance that Mother wasn't home. Seven people were standing outside on the stoop and on the garden path.

"May we come in for a moment, please?"

The doctor had a large Band-aid on his cheek. The cobbler, eyes dancing with mischief in his bearded face, stood there with head hunched between his shoulders. Selina kept to the rear of the group, looking with a touch of mockery over the shoulder of one of the glamorous ladies, who for her part was giving Chris peculiar glances out of glistening eyes. The other glamorous lady, with her carefully made-up face under silky hair piled high on her head, was also there. And the group had been joined by two other women. They were somewhat older and had kindly, motherly faces.

"May we come in, please."

What do you do in such a case if you're a little boy? Chris took a step backward and gestured toward the living room. But by the time five of the visitors had filed in, Chris had thought of a strategy. As soon as they were all inside, he would slam the living-room door shut and beat it out of the house. His mother, of course, would be upset that he had let strangers into the house. But if she'd stay around home it wouldn't have happened; she had only herself to blame.

The doctor stood aside, letting all the women and the cobbler precede him. Before Chris had a chance to carry out his plan, he again felt that strong grip on his arm.

"We've brought you your bicycle. Show me where to put it."

"Oh, I keep it in the back," Chris said hopefully. Once he had his hands on the bike he'd give the doctor a kick or punch him so hard he'd need another bandage. If only he still had his stone he could bewitch the doctor so he'd think all his bones were broken and he was lying in the hospital wrapped in plaster like a mummy. But the stone was gone, the doctor was big and strong, and Chris had no choice but to go tamely inside with him. All those faces in the living room turned to stare at him in a friendly and slightly pitying way.

"I suspect you have an entirely wrong idea about us," the doctor said. "First we want to tell you who and what we are."

Chris squirmed in his chair. He looked shyly from one to the other.

"In the first place we are normal human beings, men and women with ordinary jobs in society. In addition, we are all members of the secret society we call the Fine Thread Association. We are all practiced in a form of wisdom that goes beyond the knowledge and power of most people. It is spread like a web over the whole world. Our task is to safeguard the world. We usually do so by guiding thoughts, just at a crucial point, only when it's necessary, or by numbing a hand or keeping a voice from speaking out. One of us is on the watch wherever the world is in danger. Here is Selina, who paints portraits and puts her ideas across while people are sitting for her, quiet and relaxed. These lovely ladies are Kiki and Amanda. Powerful industrialists and statesmen come to visit them and without realizing it go away with good thoughts. Madame Farsight sits on boards of directors and boards of trustees. Madame Skein is a schoolteacher. Toontje, the cobbler, mends shoes for people and has far more influence than anyone suspects—as does our friend Fleurtje, who says almost nothing but pours out her serene goodness along with the beer in her little café. I myself reach many sick people. And there are others, many others."

Chris became more and more restless. Talk all you like, he thought. I don't have to listen. You have no business here with your secret wisdom and your serene goodness.

But he did not dare say that aloud, and the doctor continued. "I see you've learned to crochet. So perhaps you have already learned the first rudiments of our language, which we use to communicate with one another over the whole world. Most of the people who do our work are women. That's just how it happens. Men do the acting and women carry on the wisdom of humanity. But one of our wisest and most respected women has chosen for her successor someone who is going to be a man—you. We don't want to interfere with her choice. In her time she was one of the greatest among us, partly because of her personality, partly because of a talisman she possessed: the magic stone. There are a number of these things: the staff that can make dried wood sprout; the water ball, a sphere of liquid that stays together and shows the future; the

weavers, a certain type of spider raised in the east and west that can transmit messages by weaving webs in a pattern peculiar to their species. These things frequently stay in the hands of one family and are handed down to younger generations along with the secret knowledge. Sister Southwind possessed the stone that sends out rays that can pierce through the walls of a mind. Our association takes the view that she may hand the stone on to someone who has proved himself worthy of it. You have been chosen. Once your training is finished, we will take pleasure in welcoming you into our association. But until then you must give up the stone."

Chris was still huddled in his chair. They were all looking at him. He had to do something or say something.

"I've already thought of that myself," Chris said. "I gave the stone back to Grandmother. You may mean well, but I'm not getting mixed up with witchcraft."

For a moment there was an icy silence. Then the doctor said, "Do you think you can make fools of us?"

"I just don't have the stone. Search my room if you don't believe me."

"It's true," Selina said. "He doesn't have it. I feel that."

"Then we can go."

One by one they stood up.

"So long, Chris, be seeing you," Amanda said.

"I'd like another talk with you one of these days," Toontje said.

The others gave him friendly nods, even Selina.

"All good wishes," the doctor said. He was the last to leave the house.

Chris ran to the window to watch them depart, and as he watched he congratulated himself. "That was a neat fib. Grandmother doesn't have the stone either. The crow picked it up. What fun."

What would a bird do with it anyhow? Had the crow swallowed it? Then the walls of its mind would break. Would the crow go crazy? Just as crazy as that whole bunch?

Chris laughed out loud. He felt free of a tremendous pressure. It was true that these people had unusual powers, magical powers. And now they were all going on to see Grandmother. Maybe their number had already swelled to ten. More and more were coming all the time, and all of them wanted to have that stone. Grandmother had said so herself. He began to feel distinctly uneasy. He had said that she had the magic stone back, but that wasn't true. He had fibbed because he didn't want the witches to know the truth and also because it made him feel clever to fool them all. But now that whole gang would naturally descend on Grandmother. And she wouldn't be able to defend herself against so many. She was old and couldn't run away. It must take her at least half an hour to get out the door with her wheelchair, and there was nobody at home to help her.

With a frightful feeling of guilt Chris pictured the tiny figure up there in her easy chair in that room full of dressers and needlework, with all the witch people gathered around her. They'd plague her until they knew for sure that she did not have the stone, and then they'd come back to him. Maybe there would be twenty of them by then. By that time Mother would probably be home, but she wouldn't be amused to find twenty-five witches in her living room. He couldn't do that to his mother. And what would happen if they became really furious with him?

"There's nothing else to do," Chris said to himself. "I guess I have to go away with Grandmother."

Slowly he put on his jacket. He went upstairs for his toothbrush and scribbled a note: "I'm going away with Frank's grandmother for a few days after all. Don't worry." He laid this note on the table, then went out of the house by way of the back door. He took his bike and set out for Frank's house. There was a strong wind, and it was already growing dark. Chris took a shortcut along a path that was not supposed to be used for bicycle riding. It was littered with dry leaves.

Maybe he would be too late. In that case there would

be nothing to do. But maybe he would be lucky. He remembered the alley that led to the kitchen door. The light in the kitchen was on, but nobody was there. Chris entered the house and went down the dark hallway. There stood the wheelchair with Grandmother's satchel still on the seat. He heard voices and a quiet tinkle of silverware. Of course, they were having their dinner. Suddenly he felt acutely embarrassed, like an intruder. Shouldn't he go away? Maybe the witch people wouldn't come at all, or else Grandmother would just laugh at them. He was always overestimating their power.

The door opened. Frank's mother appeared with a pile of dishes. "Chris! So you're here. Come in, my boy."

Now he could no longer run away, but what should he say? Everyone in the brightly lit room was looking at him, including Grandmother, and her look was very friendly.

"They came," Chris said. "There were seven of them."

"Seven." Grandmother nodded with satisfaction. "Were you alone?"

"Yes. I thought maybe they'd come here, and Mother is away."

"Your mother was here half an hour ago. She must be home by now. Have you eaten?"

"No, I was too upset. I thought I had to warn you."

"What are you talking about?" Frank's father asked. "They—who is this they?"

"Never mind," Grandmother said. "He's had a fright. Give the child something to eat. Then I'll take him straight home."

"But, Mother, I can just as well do that, can't I?"

"Out of the question," Frank's father said. "If someone is to take him home, I'll do it."

A chair was moved and a place set for Chris. Frank kept staring at him, and Chris felt foolish. They must think him a scaredy-cat who had to have his mother around all the time.

When they were finished eating, Grandmother said, "Come." She hobbled to the wheelchair, and all the members of the family who wanted to take Chris home had to help push her outside and then go back in again.

"Nice to have some fresh air after dinner. I should do this more often."

Chris walked alongside.

"Jump up on the footboard," she commanded after a while. "We still have quite a way to go."

"But we're going to my house, aren't we?"

"Of course not." She chuckled. "You know perfectly well what I have in mind for you."

Do I know? Chris asked himself. He thought of Doctor Onkel's fancy phrases, "You have been chosen," and "in her time she was one of the greatest among us." But he didn't want any part of it; he didn't want to practice witchcraft, and he didn't want to help save the world. Leave that to those weirdies who had been pestering him all afternoon. Why, oh why, had he got himself into this mess all over again? Maybe she would no longer want him if she knew that the stone was really lost for good. He kept silent for some time, but at last he said, "A big black crow swallowed the stone."

"Did it?" she said indifferently. "I imagine it will turn up again."

The wheelchair was steadily moving faster. Grandmother's white hair fluttered in the wind and her eyes gleamed, big and black.

"Are we going to the station?" Chris asked.

"No, I've thought of a much better plan."

They were riding down a long, straight street with a great deal of traffic. They rode over a bridge and came to a rotary. Now they were almost out of the city. Grandmother let go of the handles, which continued to pump away of their own accord while the wheelchair slowed. They came to a stop at the edge of a highway.

"We're going to hitchhike," Grandmother said.

For the time being she made no attempt to flag any car. She just sat quietly, and Chris stood next to her. The wind tugged at his jacket. The big street lights above his head swayed back and forth, and the black pouch of the wheelchair rattled.

"A storm," Grandmother said. "And a new moon besides. Nice weather for witches. This kind of night is good for learning to fly. If there's anything I regret, it's that I didn't start that young enough. When I tried it with the broom I was much too old, and in a city you haven't got enough room. The association forbids it, you know. All the good old magic arts are forbidden because we're supposed to pretend we don't exist. Stupid rules. But where we're going now it's better. I have a friend who used to be a member of the association, but they expelled her because she enjoyed her work too much. Now she lives alone in a forest, and she can do tremendous things. She'll help us."

She sat quietly in the wheelchair for a while. Chris was starting to feel cold, but he felt a bit better about this excursion. Learning to fly seemed pretty good.

"Now," Grandmother said, raising her cane into the air, "wave your arms."

Chris waved, and an enormous truck slowed down with screaming brakes and came to a halt on the shoulder of the road. Behind it were two long trailers on what looked like dozens of wheels. Letters about a yard high on the side of the truck read *Furniture*. A man opened the door of the cab and jumped down. He greeted them with something that sounded like "Good evening" and went to the rear. Grandmother had set her wheelchair in motion as the truck stopped, and she now arrived at the rear door. The driver unlatched the long iron bar that locked the back of the trailer. A door opened. The driver pulled out a long steel plate so that it formed a ramp to the ground. Then he disappeared inside and brought out an odd little cart on rubber wheels. He guided it down the steel plate and rolled it to the front of the truck, while Grandmother followed in her chair. At the cab she stepped cautiously out of her wheelchair and onto the small cart. The driver began pumping something on the underside of the cart with his foot. At each step the cart rose slightly; it was a kind of jack. In a little while it was level with the door, and Grandmother was able to get into the cab without much difficulty.

The driver let the jack down and rolled it to the back door of the trailer. He said something to Chris, but Chris could not understand him. Then he took Grandmother's wheelchair and began wheeling it up the steel plate. Chris helped him push.

The trailer seemed to contain nothing but a few rolled-up rugs and a great many ropes. With much clanging and thumping the trailer was closed again, and Chris followed the driver back to the cab. The man lifted him so that he could jump inside. There was plenty of space; the cab was a pleasant little room decked out with pictures of girls and dogs and horses. A vase held a bunch of dried heather, and above the windshield hung a little crocheted curtain.

"He's one of us," Grandmother whispered.

They started off. How high above the road they were.

Grandmother began a lively conversation with the driver. But Chris did not understand a word; they were speaking German. For a while he wondered where they were going. Then he slumped back comfortably and went to sleep.

CHAPTER IX

Janna and Her Crows

Doctor Onkel and his band had arrived in Fleurtje's café. An old man with very bright eyes and a snowy beard was already there, as were the two women whom Chris had seen in the park after he had been a bird.

Only Selina did not join them. She had returned home to see whether the crow might have come to her studio. Restlessly she paced the room, for the bird was not there. She might just as well have gone to the café. But something seemed to be holding her back; she had no idea what it was. She opened and closed drawers, cleared away pencils, meanwhile slipping on her green crocheted stole. At last the crow announced itself by tapping at the windowpane. The window had been left partly open all day long, and the bird pushed its way in before Selina had a chance to open it any farther. Had the crow carried out her orders?

The bird swooped to the same chairback as before, with more than its usual look of impudence, but it had nothing in its beak. Then it flew to the low chest on which the blue bowl stood. Something dark and glistening lay in the bowl. Selina saw at once what it was and cried out in her excitement. There was the stone; the crow must have brought it earlier.

"You dear crow!" Selina exclaimed joyfully.

"Caw, caw," the crow replied, and before Selina could do a thing it picked up the stone and flew out the window.

"Come here," Selina shouted, "come back, you wretched crow. Give me that stone!"

"Haw-haw," came the bird's call far away over the roofs.

Selina was stunned. She paced back and forth in her attic studio, rearranging things that might just as well have stayed where they were. Finally she decided to go to the café after all, since there was no longer any chance for her to get the stone for herself and she wanted to know what plans the others were making.

She descended the three long flights of stairs to the outside. The wind blew right through her crocheted stole and whipped her red hair about like a flag. Selina shivered, but she strode straight into the wind for about twenty minutes until she reached the gray café with the dirty windowpanes on the seedy little street. Inside, nothing was dirty at all. Fleurtje kept her place neat and sparkling. The thick spider webs on the windowpanes served only to keep strangers away. Inside, the café was crowded and friendly.

Almost the entire membership of the association was meeting to talk about Sister Southwind, her stone, and the little boy she had chosen for her successor. But the only thing to be said on that matter was: the stone in the hands of a child was a danger to the world. That had been said before, and there the matter rested because witches do not use force. Moreover, a few members had come from far away and they had no real interest in the problem. There were sailors from Ireland, young red-haired men full of magic arts and full of music as well. One of them had brought an accordion, and they sang songs as was their custom at home and in cafés. So it was not a serious conference Selina found, but a party.

Fleurtje was kept busy serving both beer and herb tea. She kept trotting back into the kitchen where her kettle sat on the stove. There the wind howled in the chimney, and she could hear the rattle of a piece of loose guttering that had almost blown off. Fleurtje pressed the hearing-aid switch that was concealed inside her blouse and took the pink hearing aid out of her ear. Then everything was pleasantly quiet. Noise always bothered her, whether it was the wind in the guttering or twenty people all talking at once. The Irish boys sang nicely enough, but Fleurtje couldn't understand their language.

Selina, an absent expression on her face, had found a place in a corner. Toontje the cobbler brought over a chair and sat down at her table. "Hi, Selina, where have you been all this time?"

"Home," Selina said. She drank from her glass and lapsed into silence.

"What's eating you?" Toontje inquired.

"I had the magic stone and now it's gone."

"You don't say."

"I sent out one of my birds, a crow. I told it to go to such and such a neighborhood and bring me the stone. Meanwhile, the rest of us were trying our luck with that boy. But there at the school yard I saw the crow hanging around. So I thought, You never know, the bird might manage to get hold of it. Better go home and await developments."

"We missed you here."

"Nothing seemed to be happening at the studio, but I had the feeling something would. Then the crow came flying in again and showed me the stone in the blue tea bowl. It must have been there all the while, but I hadn't seen it."

"And now it's gone?"

"The crow flew away with it. This wasn't an ordinary crow. I can make birds do anything, but this one knows its own mind. And now the magic stone is lost forever. We can't possibly search all the crows' nests in the region."

"Sounds bad," Toontje agreed.

An old man with a snow-white beard was sitting near them. "Crows," he quavered. "We used to have Janna and her crows. If it wasn't an ordinary crow, it must have been one of Janna's."

"This is the first I've heard of them," Selina said. "Who was this Janna?"

"Tell us about it," Toontje urged.

The old man gazed into space with eyes almost devoid of color. "There were two of them to begin with," he said. "Janna and Tanna. Two wild girls. All the fellows were crazy about them. Janna came from somewhere in the east, and Tanna was born right here in this city. But Tanna also had witchcraft in her blood. She came from a very old family that had passed the magic arts on from daughter to daughter. The girls had rich friends. What parties they used to give! And if they had had a mind to marry, they could have had their choice. But they didn't want to. They weren't interested in men of position, and they didn't want any of us ordinary fellows either. One day they just cleared out of the city, went along with the circus. Tanna did equestrian tricks, leaping from one horse's back to another's, turning somersaults, and no matter what, always managing to fix her black eyes on the audience. And Janna did an act with her trained crows. Those crows of hers could do anything; they were almost human. Janna would say, 'See, over there in the fourth row is a gentleman with a pretty tiepin. Bring me that.' And the crow would fly to the fourth row and pluck the pin out of the man's tie. Of course people would get back their valuables after the show. When the circus came to town, we all went and lined up in the front row, flashing gold buttons and silver pencils and hoping that Janna would send one of her crows to us. . . . Yes, yes, those were the days. You don't find girls like that anymore. I wonder what's become of her."

"Why, Sybren," an old woman said. "Tanna came back here later and married. Didn't you know that?"

"No," the white-haired man said. "Never heard a thing about it."

"She married a dull, ordinary man, not a member of our association. But she's very much part of it herself. She's Sister Southwind, who's the cause of all this trouble we're having."

"Sister Southwind? She sure has changed a lot. Well, maybe not so much after all. We always used to have trouble with her. With her and Janna. Those two just couldn't help it. They loved trouble, Janna and Tanna."

"You live and learn," Toontje the cobbler murmured. "Janna and her crows, and Tanna. Maybe we ought to call the meeting to order. Where is Doctor Onkel?"

The heavy trailer truck thundered across the countryside, and Chris slept on, quite comfortable on the front seat between the truck driver and Grandmother. It was about one o'clock in the morning when they arrived at their destination. During the last part of their trip the truck had been on a road for which it was really too big, but they met no traffic in the other direction. Now they stopped.

There was a large, rusty iron gate before them, flanked with trees whose branches were whipping in the wind. The gate was closed with a padlock. Chris, who had slumped way down in the seat, started awake. The driver had left the cab and was gone for some time.

"Where are we?"

"Close to the German border. There's a small castle here where nobody lives, and a farmstead that belongs to the place. Behind the farmhouse they've built cottages for summer boarders. The forest around here is very old."

"Why does nobody live in the castle?"

"Because it's bewitched, of course." Grandmother laughed.

"And the summer cottages?"

"It's not summer anymore. In all probability the cottages will be empty. We only need one. The driver is arranging all that for us. He's had to rout the farmer out of bed."

"That's very nice of him, isn't it? I guess he's gone out of his way for us."

"I should say he has, but of course it was the way he had to go."

Chris did not understand that statement very well. He waited. A swaying light appeared. The driver opened the cab door and called up something unclear. Not only the foreign language but the noise of the wind made it incomprehensible.

"We have to get out," Grandmother said.

Chris jumped down. The spot where he landed was sandy; he fell and staggered to his feet again. At the rear of the truck the driver was once more busy with iron rods and doors. Then he came up with the jack. It proved to be more difficult to get Grandmother out of the truck than it had been to get her in, for it was dark and there was little room in which to place the wheelchair. But at last they had her firmly seated.

They thanked the driver warmly. He climbed back

into his cab as nimbly as a monkey and started the motor. Very slowly the huge vehicle began to move off, and when all the big letters were past Chris realized that he did not even know what the man looked like. Chris had to open the gate, then close it and take the key out of the padlock. They were now in a driveway lined by oak trees. The high wind whirled up vast numbers of dried leaves.

The building before them was totally dark. In the farmhouse a small light burned behind a low window. Two dogs barked madly. Now they came to a sandy path where Chris had to push hard to propel the wheelchair. And there before them was a cottage, a tiny building with a peaked roof and a front door that had little squares of glass in it.

"The third house," Grandmother said. Vigorously she pulled at the handles, and Chris pushed from behind.

After a turn in the path they reached the third cottage. Chris had to open it with a different key. Grandmother wanted to ride straight in, wheelchair and all, but that proved impossible. The door was too narrow. After a good deal of struggling with the canes, while the wind nearly blew her over, she made it inside at last.

It was cold in the room. Chris could not resist looking inside all the cupboards. There were pots, plates, and cups, but not a thing to eat. The cottage had one bedroom with bunk beds. These beds had blankets but no sheets, and there were no towels either. A thin stream of water ran from the faucet above the sink.

"Tomorrow we'll get straightened out," Grandmother said. "At the moment what we chiefly need is sleep. You can lie down over there."

Built in between the table and the window was a bench that could also serve as a couch. Grandmother hobbled into the bedroom at the back of the cottage.

"Here, take another blanket."

Chris lay down on the bench. He kept his clothes on. How odd the blankets smelled. He had not known that a wind could make such a racket in a forest. What did it mean when a castle was bewitched? With such thoughts in his head it was a long time before he fell asleep.

Next morning the sun shone in through the window. The wind was still blowing, but not so hard. The noise the wind was making now had something festive about it, and specks of sunlight danced about the room as the trees swayed in the wind. The play of sun and shadow gave the room a cheerful look.

Chris lay in bed watching the spectacle and trying to figure out which branches cast which shadows.

From the tiny bedroom came a thump. Could Grandmother have fallen from that narrow bunk?

"Chris, Chris, come and help me."

Sure enough. Unwillingly Chris crawled out of the blankets and stepped into his shoes. With trailing laces he made for the bedroom.

"That's the way it is," Grandmother said. "There are things I no longer can do, but on the other hand I can still do lots of things that most people will never be able to do no matter how long they live. Pick up that chair."

Grandmother had not fallen. She was sitting on the edge of the lower bunk in a flowered nightgown, her white hair hanging in thin strands over her shoulders.

Chris set the chair straight. Then he had to gather up everything that had tumbled to the floor: a satin slip, black stockings, and embroidered bloomers. He thought it a little odd to be handling these things but did his best not to show his feelings.

Her satchel had also spilled. Grandmother had taken more with her than just a toothbrush. On the floor lay a comb and a packet of soap. Chris wondered whether he was supposed to get along for a whole week without a comb.

"Where should I wash up?"

"Go and look around. I've never been here either. But wait till I'm ready. I can do everything by myself, but it takes awhile, and I'd just as soon you were nearby in case something else happens like that chair falling over. Meanwhile, you can think out what we're going to need—bread and eggs and things like that."

Chris found it very hard to think that out; he had never kept house before. He went into the little kitchen to wash his face. Maybe there would be a shed with showers outside, the way there was at a camping site.

When Grandmother was ready—her black dress neatly buttoned, her hair gathered in a bun—she sent him into the bedroom for her handbag. Then she gave him money and told him to go to the farmhouse.

"Ask them for milk and bread. Oh, yes, and towels and bed linen—and onions. You can do all sorts of things with onions."

The dogs started barking as soon as Chris stepped outside. They were probably real watchdogs, and he was a stranger. Luckily, he was not afraid. Chris walked straight toward them, calling out at each step, "Down, down now!"

The dogs were Alsatians. They ran toward him and then retreated. Their teeth glistened, huge and white in their black jaws, but they did not bite.

At last someone came out, a tall woman wearing a blue apron. She called out something, but he could not make out what it was. She spoke a dialect, and Chris could hardly understand a word of it. But she understood him quite well, and she was able to make clear how much he had to pay for the things she gave him.

Back at the cottage he helped Grandmother make tea and fry eggs. For the first time he began to feel that he was enjoying himself. Certainly he wasn't sorry about missing school.

"And now we'll go to see my old friend," Grandmother said.

By this point Chris was in a happy mood and looking forward eagerly to developments. He rolled the wheelchair close to the door and swept away the dried leaves. Grandmother hobbled over to the door and sniffed the fresh air appreciatively. By daylight Chris could plainly see where the ruts were in the gravel road. He steered the wheelchair away from them, but otherwise it was no strain to keep it going. With only a little shove now and then it went almost by itself.

The road wound along some ten cottages. Then came a fork, and they turned into the woods. There everything was suddenly much quieter. The wind shook only the topmost branches, and a dim filtered light prevailed. To either side of the road stood tall plants with fluffy seedpods and blackened leaves. But Chris also noticed bushes that were still entirely green, and there were even some little yellow flowers amid the grass. It was not winter yet.

"The forest is feeling good after the storm," Grandmother said. "Blown clean."

"How can a forest have feelings?" Chris asked.

"Everything that lives has feelings. Don't you know that? I have to teach you a great deal, and I think I may as well begin right away."

She let go of the handles and the wheelchair stopped. So did Chris. He waited for Grandmother to say something, but she said nothing, just looked around and seemed to be listening. Chris listened with her. He heard the wind, which now was merely soughing, and now and then something rustling. Somewhere a bird flew up, but not a creature was singing, peeping, or whistling. After they had kept still for a while, Chris felt that he somewhat understood what Grandmother meant. Although they were under the trees, he had a feeling of freshness and openness. He was well aware that a forest could feel very oppressive at times. So this open feeling must have been caused by last night's storm.

"You've learned to see all there is as things," Grandmother said. "A house is a thing, a tree is a thing, and you yourself are a thing with arms and legs and eyes with which to look at other things. But there is another way to think about the world. When we talk together we give something to each other. Something of me has gone into you, and something of you has come to me."

Grandmother paused to collect her thoughts. "And a great deal also depends on where you are. Chris alone in the dark is different from Chris in the classroom.

Chris in the woods can feel how the forest feels. Every tree has its own feelings. In living things that stay in one place, the collective feeling is stronger than the individual feeling, and so a forest has power. The magic stone admits you into the feelings of another person, but you have access to those feelings even without the stone. Very small children feel in the same way as trees in the woods. It takes awhile before they become individuals. Everybody keeps some of that ability to feel collectively. Can you understand that it is sad, and dangerous as well, for someone not to recognize his connections with things, to think that he has no influence over them, to believe he can't affect them?"

"No," Chris said, "I can't understand it because I really *can't* affect them."

"When you went to the farmhouse and the dogs retreated, you went ahead more than you would have done if you had thought you were a powerless thing."

"Oh," Chris said.

"Exactly," Grandmother said. "That was the first lesson."

She took hold of the handles and set off again. Chris pushed a little and thought about what she had said. It was not a disagreeable idea that he was more important than he had always imagined. If you looked at things the way Grandmother did, you might well become the most important person in the world. Chris took a deep breath, so that he would be able to absorb the feelings of all the things flying around in the air. The forest was a power and so was he. But then he thought he had better be careful, for hadn't she said, "when we talk together we give something to each other." All very well and good, but he was not of a mind to change himself. He wanted to keep a very close watch on himself and his thoughts because he wanted to remain the master of them.

In silence, they went on. A rabbit ran across the road, and twice they saw pheasants. And then the crow appeared.

"Oh, look," Chris said, "I think it's the same crow. Or are crows so much alike that you can't tell them apart?"

The bird sat on a low branch of a fir tree, and it did not fly off when they passed close by. A short distance farther on, still another crow was perched.

The first bird began to caw in the same mocking way as that other crow had done, and again Chris had the idea that he knew it. The second crow took up the cry. "Haw-haw-haw-haw!" They were being laughed at.

Then Grandmother called out, "Go and tell her that we're on the way."

Cawing, the birds took wing.

"Can they understand you?" Chris asked. But sure enough, she was a witch. Maybe she knew bird language. Would she be willing to teach it to him? That would be a lot more fun than the strange lesson she'd given him awhile back.

"They can't understand the words," Grandmother said. "But they know what I mean because I was close to them. They live with my old friend. But she already knows that I'm coming, because I've been close to her these past few days."

"And is that magic?"

"What makes you think that? There's no such thing as magic. Those who say that are right enough. But most people are so stupid that they deny the existence of everything they can't understand. Or they call it chance. It's just like telephoning, except you don't need an instrument. Everybody who doesn't think he's a thing should be able to do it."

"Oh, and flying on a broom must be just the same as using an airplane except you don't need any gasoline."

Chris spoke sarcastically, but Grandmother took up the question with lively interest. "Exactly. How else do you think I'd be able to ride so easily along this bumpy gravel road?"

"On witch power," Chris mumbled, and Grandmother laughed, not as hoarsely as the crows, but still she sounded rather spooky.

"Do we have far to go?" Chris asked. He was thinking, How big this forest is; without witch power I would never get out of it. The ground underfoot was firm, but there no longer seemed to be anything like a road or path. Was this the time he would discover what it was like to be afraid?

Still, it smelled good among the fir trees. The sky was almost cloudless now, and the splashes of sunlight fell warmly upon the two of them as they went deeper into the woods. Discovering fear could wait awhile. Here the trees were no longer so dense. There were more birches and other kinds of trees. And then, to his surprise, Chris saw a small tree weighed down with red apples.

A different kind of smell tickled his nostrils. Fragrant plants were growing here, but there was also a smell of burning. He saw smoke in the distance. Grandmother had not replied, but he realized that they were now almost at their destination.

They passed a woodpile, and Chris saw a red cabbage that just grew right out of the grass. When he looked around he saw that they were now in a kind of vegetable garden, for other vegetables were growing there, but all mixed up and nothing in a row.

Behind the woodpile stood five beehives. From that point he could see the bonfire and the little woman who stood by it. She was poking in the flames with a long stick, so that sparks shot high up into the smoke. She did not look up. Even when they were close to her, she continued to stare obstinately into the fire.

She was somewhat smaller than Grandmother. Her eyes were narrowed almost to slits, which made her look thoroughly mischievous, and she appeared to have not a tooth in her mouth. Suddenly she threw a handful of leaves into the flames. The same fragrance that Chris had noticed before came from the fire, but now it was heavy and acrid. Again she poked with her stick, and this time she cast a sidelong glance at Grandmother. Suddenly both old women began to laugh, Grandmother in her usual tittering way, "Hee-hee-hee," and the other woman with her head thrown back and her toothless mouth wide open, "Heh-heh-heh-heh." Chris was completely unnerved. What a weird pair they were!

CHAPTER X

The Rain Barrel

After this peculiar form of greeting, Grandmother introduced him. "This is Chris."

The toothless old woman threw the stick aside and took his hand. "Come along, child."

She led him to a tall hedge. Grandmother followed in her wheelchair. They went through an opening in the hedge, and there stood a tiny farmhouse, broad and low, with a thatched roof. Next to it was a well, and on a pole was exactly the same house in miniature, on which a number of pigeons were sitting. All around were fruit trees and berry bushes, and the yard was alive with promenading geese, scampering kittens, and scratching hens.

"A lovely place you have here, Janna," Grandmother

exclaimed, and Janna again showed her pleasure by opening her mouth wide.

Now Grandmother had to abandon her wheelchair and hobble in on her two canes. Janna stood watching, shaking her head. Then she suddenly snatched up a broom and held it out to Grandmother. Both of them began to hiccup from laughter. Chris was still not feeling altogether at ease.

They entered a kitchen with a stone floor and roughly plastered walls. The table was made of heavy planks. Janna began to cut thick slices of brown bread and to set out butter, cheese, and honey. Obviously she intended them to eat, although it was still early in the morning. Chris had a good appetite after the long walk in the woods, but it was odd that all this took place in total silence.

After a while he noticed that the two women were in fact conducting a kind of conversation. Now and then one of them nodded or shook her head, and then the two would laugh at the same time.

After the meal Janna lit a pipe, and Grandmother said, "Why don't you go outside, Chris? I have a great deal to say, and it's boring for you. There's plenty to see around here."

And Janna added, "Pick yourself a juicy apple, child."

Chris obediently went out, although he was actually

rather curious about the conversation between the witches. First he looked at the bonfire. It had almost gone out. He walked around the house. There was a pasture on the other side, and a cow was sitting just inside the enclosure. He had never been so close to a cow before. How fearfully big its head was. The slavering mouth went back and forth, back and forth. Chewing its cud—he knew at once that it was chewing its cud. At school they taught you that cows did this, and it was true.

Pleased with himself, he went on exploring the place. The well was also enormous. Deep, deep down he saw the water, and it gave back a hollow sound when he shouted, "Boo." A pail hung from a chain that was wound around a heavy shaft. At the end of the shaft was an iron handle. Chris turned the handle and let the pail down slowly. Plump! Then he began drawing it up again. This was fun, but it must be a nuisance if it was the only way to get water.

There was also a huge rain barrel nearby. Chris went over to it and lifted the lid. The barrel was almost as tall as he himself was, and it was more than half full. Just as he was about to let the lid drop again, he noticed something glittering at the bottom. He tilted the lid up once again and looked more carefully. Yes, there it was, just like a tiny star. With a shock he recognized the five points of the star in the magic stone.

Chris leaned over the rim of the barrel and peered into the dark water. Was there really something lying at the bottom? He could not see it now, but when he moved his head back and forth he could detect the little star just as when he still had the stone and shifted it back and forth in his hand. Could that crow after all have been the very same one there in the woods? Maybe the crow had dropped the stone in the rain gutter, and the rain had washed it down into the barrel.

If that were so, how was he to get it out again? By now Chris was sorry he had thrown the stone away. He would go and look for something with which to fish it out of the barrel. A butterfly net would be just right. What a pity there was nothing like that around here. But there was a dipper hanging on a nail by the well. That would work, although the handle would have to be three times as long as it was.

Chris looked around for a piece of cord or wire that he could use to attach a stick to the dipper. He saw a wooden rake and a few tools he didn't recognize, but none of these things would help.

He left the yard through the opening in the hedge. Oh, yes, he was supposed to get himself an apple. He went back to the little tree that he had first noticed. Quite a few windfalls were lying on the ground under it. He ate one with big bites and started on a second.

Then he stuffed a few more apples into his pocket and went back to the house. It seemed to him that the two old ladies must have had their talk by now.

Just as he approached the house, Janna came to the doorway. This was a good example of telephoning without an instrument, Chris thought. Once inside he asked Grandmother, "Did you call me without a sound, or did you notice that I was coming back?"

"It was time," Grandmother said. "All three of us sensed that it was time. Now it's your turn."

Chris did not mention his discovery. First he took in the surroundings. They were no longer sitting in the kitchen, but in a room back of it. It was rather dark here, for the window was small and there was a tree outside. As in Grandmother's room in Frank's house, bunches of herbs were hung everywhere to dry, and there was also a strange-looking thing hanging from the ceiling. It was shaped like a lampshade, but it was made of crocheting and very artistic. There were cats and birds in the room, and on the table, which was draped with a violet cloth, stood a transparent globe. Was that the contraption with which Janna used to do such remarkable things that the other members had thrown her out of the association?

Beside her chair stood a large flowerpot, which had a stringy plant in it. Behind it was another pot with a plant that was withered and dry, really no more than a woody stalk with a couple of twigs.

"Sit down, child," Janna said.

She filled her pipe and then tapped on the flowerpot. To Chris's astonishment the woody stalk began to move. It stepped out of the soil and jumped to the floor. Running on five crooked roots, it went into the kitchen and was back a moment later. It was not a dwarf or anything like that, but a real woody stalk. Janna picked it up, and now Chris saw that the plant had fetched a coal from the kitchen stove. Janna lit her pipe with it and replanted the stalk in the pot. It wriggled a bit on its roots and then stood still.

"Well, how do you like that?" Grandmother asked.

"Does the plant like doing it?" Chris asked.

"Heh-heh-heh-heh," Janna laughed.

But Grandmother answered somewhat grumpily, "If it went against the plant's nature, Janna would never have been able to teach it a trick like that. Perhaps it doesn't always feel like doing it, but then you don't always feel like doing arithmetic."

Chris said nothing, but he thought, You don't burn your fingers doing arithmetic. And when Selina made me into a bird I didn't like that at all. I don't think a plant enjoys having to act like a servant. Chris still felt that he was against witchcraft.

The two women sensed his opposition as clearly as if he had spoken aloud, and for a moment they were silent. Then Grandmother said, "Janna, you didn't believe that I had made a good choice. What do you say now? To my mind Chris has exactly the traits that are necessary."

"Yes," Janna said, "that may well be, but she has to enjoy doing it or she'd be better off as a housewife."

"Housewife?" Chris said. "But I'm not a girl."

"Aren't you? What are you?"

"A boy, of course."

At that Janna smacked the table so hard that Chris jumped. "A boy! And you thought you'd made a good choice. Now let me tell you something, Tanna Southwind. The clumsiest woman in our profession is still way better than a man, if you want to know. A boy—bah."

"That's how it may have been in the past, but it isn't that way any longer."

"Nonsense. That's how it has always been and it isn't going to change, because human nature never changes. Men exist to work, and they're good at learning too. That's because their minds keep going stiffly and steadily in one direction. But they're never wise."

"There are a few in our association."

"A fine lot. Bunglers."

"I didn't know you had such a dislike for men, Janna."

"I don't have a dislike for them. I think they're grand, but limited. Do you know how a man looks at things? He'll choose a goal and direct his life toward it. But we follow nature and don't see the goal till later on. I wouldn't be surprised if this little fellow already has a goal."

"That's right," Chris said. "I'm going to be rich when I grow up, but I don't know how yet."

"Sure enough. Keep your eyes fastened on that goal of yours no matter what. Never mind that you're blind to everything else."

"I've been on the lookout for a successor for twenty years," Grandmother insisted, "but there was nobody until Chris came along. I know for certain that he is the right one. Incidentally, have you picked out a successor?"

"No, and I probably never will, because these last years I've never gone more than a hundred yards from my house, and nobody comes here."

"What about my sister?" Chris suggested. "She could do as a replacement for both of you. Johanna is a real witch, and she'd just love it."

Both of them cackled merrily at that. Then Grandmother said, "We'd better be starting back to the cottage. It's a long way."

Janna said nothing, and Chris gave Grandmother her canes.

Should I mention that the magic stone is in the rain barrel? Chris wondered. If I say nothing it may stay there forever, because I don't think we'll be coming here again. But I don't know what will happen if I tell.

Grandmother hobbled outside. When she was at last seated in her wheelchair, she sighed. "Thank you, Janna. I'm glad we had this chance to visit with each other again. There won't be many such chances."

Janna puckered up her face in an odd sort of way. Chris was wondering whether he too was supposed to say something polite. And what should it be?

They came to the opening in the hedge. At that point Janna reached out and gripped the back of the wheelchair. "You mustn't leave," she said. "You mustn't leave this way. We still have endless things to talk over, don't we? I don't want you to go so soon. I've been alone much too long."

"If that's how it is," Grandmother said, "we can reconsider. Chris, how do you like the idea of staying?"

"All right with me."

"Why not stay a few days? Nobody knows where you are anyhow."

"Why not?" Grandmother chuckled. "We'll give them all the slip."

Chris noticed that she had her satchel with her. "But

I don't have any clothes with me," he said. "Not even a comb. All I brought along was my toothbrush anyway, and that's back at the cottage."

Grandmother did not seem perturbed. "It was up to you to know what to take along."

"Well, you'll manage," Janna said. "For the first evening you can simply wash up with a pail at the well. I'll find you a towel."

Then she pointed out a tree with chestnuts under it. He was to remove each nut from its prickly outer husk and then make a slit in the brown, shining skin with a knife she gave him. The embers of the fire were just right for roasting the chestnuts. Grandmother was also given a knife to peel apples for applesauce, and Janna herself dug a few potatoes and picked Brussels sprouts from the plants scattered here and there. "We'll have a lovely dinner," she chortled. "And if there are enough eggs we'll even have pancakes."

Chris could not quite decide whether he liked it at Janna's. Not being able to comb his hair didn't bother him that much. But on the other hand life here was very different from the way it was at home. There was plenty to see and investigate, and he was also planning to go fishing in the rain barrel. But he did not exactly feel at ease with the two cackling old women, and when he went off by himself he felt awfully alone.

They ate early. The chestnuts turned out perfectly, soft and sweet, and the fresh-picked sprouts, which he never particularly liked at home, tasted much better here.

After the meal Janna went to milk her cow. Chris wanted to watch how she did that. She squeezed the teats that hung beneath the udder, and two jets of milk spurted alternately into the pail with a twanging sound. He was curious to see how much milk would come out, but the milking took too long and he drifted on.

Dusk was already falling. A mist hung above the little pasture, and still higher was the sun, big and orange, its lower edge swathed in cloud. In a hazel bush a few starlings were making a great fuss.

Chris roamed around and finally found a piece of wire that had come loose from the gate. One end of it was still attached to a post. Keeping an eye out for Janna, who was still milking, he started bending the wire. It was rusty and broke quickly. He meant to attach it to the dipper so that he could fish in the rain barrel.

Quickly and quietly he went around to the other side of the house. He crept behind the rain barrel to measure how long his piece of wire had to be. At the back of the barrel he saw a black thread that was caught in a splinter of the wood. It went over the edge of the barrel, and when he lifted the lid he saw that the thread ran down on the inside into the water. It did not look as if it had been there long. Chris took hold of the thread and pulled. The end under the splinter came loose. He wound the thread around his hand and cautiously drew the other end out of the water.

There was something attached to it. Even before he could see it, he knew what it was. He watched in suspense as it came to the surface. Sure enough, it was the stone, his magic stone.

It was enclosed in a little net made of the same black thread. Chris felt an odd combination of gladness and nervousness. He realized that Janna must have hidden the stone here. Now he had it again, which was fine. But how furious she would be if she knew. He tucked the stone, thread and all, deep into his pocket and had the impulse to clear out at once. Just in time he thought of the piece of wire. She must not find it here. He took it with him and went out through the opening in the hedge, away from the farmyard. Then he began running fast, past the little apple tree and into the dense thickets. There he hid behind some bushes, heart pounding.

What should he do now? If only he could go home. At this hour Mother would be attending to Johanna. She would probably be reading to her, and then Johanna would spend a quarter of an hour deciding whether to take Esmeralda or the bear to bed with her.

When he himself was small, he had always gone to bed with Tingaling. That was the rag doll with the bell in its stomach that Mother had made for him. He found himself longing for Tingaling and also for Mother and Johanna and his little desk and the tankful of fish. Would I be able to find the way back? Chris wondered. And then? He had no money for a bus or train. He didn't even know the name of this place. Maybe he could telephone from the farmhouse with the dogs and ask his parents to come for him. How great if his father came to take him home.

It was cold. The sun had nearly set by now. All he could see were a few orange streaks in the sky above the trees. Soon it would be pitch dark, and then he could easily get lost. Maybe it would be better to wait in this hiding place until tomorrow. Would Janna send her crows after him if he tried to escape? Would they peck at him until he changed direction and scurried back to the little house?

Now I am scared after all, Chris suddenly thought. I thought I never would be, but I don't dare go back to Grandmother and Janna, and I don't dare run off into the woods at night. But if I had some hope of finding the way I would, and if I thought that Janna wouldn't suspect about the stone I'd go back there. So I'm really not all that scared. I guess I'll just go back to Janna.

He hid the piece of wire in the bushes and wended his way back toward the little house. Passing the apple tree, he picked up a few more apples and munched them.

The old ladies were in the kitchen. There was a fire in the stove, and the room was good and hot.

"Well, Chris, did you take a nice evening walk? Would you like a cup of tea?"

"Yes, please," Chris said. "It smells good."

"It's made from herbs that grow around the place," Janna said. "A very special tea." She tittered, then poured a large cup of the brew and stirred in a spoonful of honey.

Chris sipped it. It had a strange taste. Darkness was rapidly falling, but the old ladies did not light any lamps. Only when Janna lifted the stove lids with the iron prong to add wood, could he see her wrinkled old face distinctly in the glow of the fire. Grandmother's face became a white spot with something sparkling in her darker eyes.

Chris felt himself getting drowsy from the warmth, the darkness, and perhaps from the tea.

"You can sleep in the loft room," Janna said. "Come along, child, and I'll show you where."

They had to pass through the room with the walking plant. Behind a door of colored glass four steps led up to the loft room. In it was a big black wardrobe and an immense bed. There were no blankets on the bed, just a kind of big cushion. Janna lit a candle that stood in front of a mirror. That way it looked as if there were two candles. She left him, and Chris undressed.

He crawled into the big bed. The sheets again had a strange smell and were somewhat coarser than at home, but the bed was very comfortable. A length of white cloth hung over the window, but it reached only halfway down and Chris could see that it was not entirely dark outside. He blew out the candle. What a strange gleam was in this little room. Everywhere he saw things edged with light—around the wardrobe, around the mirror, and around the window. What a strange room.

Was that something moving?

What a deep, deep bed.

Sleep.

CHAPTER XI

The Pigsty

Chris awakened to the clanking of pails. With a start he sat up and at once thought of the magic stone. He had undressed, had left the stone in his pocket, and gone to sleep. How could he have been so stupid? He snatched up his trousers and felt them. The stone was still there, luckily, still in its net made of thread.

Outside someone was splashing water. Was Janna busy at the rain barrel? Then she would notice that the thread was missing. Again he had been stupid. He should have left the thread there or hung another pebble of the same size from it. Then she might have thought the stone was still undisturbed.

I want to get away, Chris thought. I want like anything to get away from here. I'm scared of Janna.

It was very early, not even full daylight yet. Outside a cat sat by the window. The window reached right down to the floor. The cat was looking at him. He hastily got into his clothes and went to the door with the colored panes of glass. The cat jumped off the windowsill and trotted away.

Very quietly Chris opened the door. Where could Grandmother be? Still sound asleep? It would not be very nice to skip out without saying thank you or good-bye. But as he thought this his glance fell upon the woody stalk, and his scruples vanished. The poor plant that had to bring red-hot coals for Janna. Anyone who made a plant carry out such orders was cruel and heartless.

I'll take it with me, Chris thought. At home I'll put it in the sun and give it extra care. He picked up the plant, pot and all. In his other hand he was holding his shoes. I'll go to the stables and get horse manure, he thought. With its soil enriched the poor plant will start to grow and leaf out.

For a full minute he listened at the kitchen door. But all was quiet. If he were lucky, Janna would be milking her cow now, and he would be a good distance away before she missed him.

He opened the door, and sure enough there was no one in the kitchen. But the kettle was on the stove, singing a merry song. Chris put on his shoes and went outside. He looked around. The yard was strangely deserted. Apparently the geese and chickens were not yet awake. There was a mist, and every leaf and blade of grass glistened with dew. The two crows perched in a plum tree were so very still that not a drop of dew fell from the glistening, wet spider webs on the tree. Chris walked calmly out through the opening in the hedge, just as he had done yesterday, but once he was out he began to run.

"You don't have to be afraid," he murmured to the woody stalk in the little pot. "You can come with me, and I'll take good care of you and talk to you a lot."

At that point he stumbled and fell with such a thump that the flowerpot smashed and the leafless plant flew a yard away. Stunned, he looked around. In the grass lay the piece of wire he had hidden yesterday. And from behind the bushes Janna appeared.

"Oh, child," she said sweetly, "did you fall?" She took hold of his wrist and helped him to his feet. "Come along, child."

Chris did not want to come, but she had him firmly in her grip. She dragged him along behind her, back through the hedge and to the rear of the yard where there was a large barn that Chris had not yet investigated. She pulled him into the barn through a narrow doorway.

Chris struggled harder and began calling out, "Help, Grandmother, help!"

He was dragged past a wooden wagon on high wheels. Janna opened a little door and pushed him into a pen. Clap, the door shut, and there he sat on ground covered with straw.

There was no window in the pen, but on one side the partition did not reach to the ceiling. If he pulled himself up, he could peer over the wall.

He heard strange noises, and there was a terrible stench. With some difficulty he hitched himself up along the partition until he could see what was on the other side. Immediately he let himself drop back into the straw. Right alongside was a pen just like the one he was in, with a pig as big as a whale inside it. That pen had a window.

I was right, Chris thought. Janna is a person to be scared of. What does she intend to do with me? And what should I do to get out of here? The door was good and solid; he had already tried it. The window in the other sty was too small for him to crawl through, and Chris had no idea whether the pig was a friendly beast. For the present he didn't mean to find out by paying the pig a visit. He had his stone. He would try to call Grandmother with it. That ought to work. He went over to a corner and sat down, holding the magic stone tightly. Grandmother, come and help me. I can't get out. Grandmother, ride your wheelchair over to the big barn. Help me, help me!

In between Chris also thought of his mother and father. Mother, I want to go home. Father, come for me. I'm locked up by a wicked witch. Father, Grandmother, help me.

After half an hour he heard a thumping. Was that Grandmother? Had she felt his call? It was Janna. She had brought him a pancake with honey and a cup of milk.

"I don't want anything to eat. I want to be let out."

"Certainly," she said. "But not right now. Later."

"Why the pancake? Do you want to fatten me? Do you want to eat me up?"

Janna laughed so hard she began to hiccup. "No, no, I only want you to enjoy yourself here. But you must give me the stone."

Chris jumped up and tried to rush past her. She's a little thing, he thought; I'll just knock her down. But he had no luck. Janna wore long, wide skirts, three or four on top of each other, and he was caught by them.

"I had it hidden so nicely," Janna said. "I thought you would never find it. Then it would be mine. But partly I hoped that you would find it, because if you took it, that would make you a thief. And you wanted to steal my fetch-and-carry plant besides. That makes you a thief twice over. So I've locked you up as you deserve, but not forever. Once Tanna Southwind is gone and I have the stone, I'll make you forget the path through the woods. Then you can help me around the farm. I'll teach you how to milk the cow and extract honey and many other things."

"And I'll never be allowed to go home again?"

"Oh, yes, but when you're in the city you'll long to be back here. You'll long for the morning mist and the smell of hay, for buttercups and violets and the first apples in the fall. You'll even long for the cooing of the pigeons and the call of the cuckoo, though those are annoying sounds. And you won't let anything on earth keep you from returning to the little house in the woods. I know it, because that's just how it's been for me. You'll even long for me, though at the moment you don't like me at all. And when I die, everything will be yours. You'll inherit the whole place."

"I don't want to inherit anything," Chris said.

"Oh, yes, this is just what you wanted even before you ever set eyes on the place."

"I'm not giving up the stone."

"Then keep it awhile longer. It won't help you. Eat your pancake while it's warm; it tastes better that way." Janna slid the big bolt on the door and left the barn.

At that moment Grandmother came hobbling out of the house on her two canes. "Good morning, Janna. How early you're up."

"I'm an early riser. I've milked the cow and fed the pig. And how did you sleep on my mattress stuffed with fresh fern?"

"I had a deep sleep. What did you put in the tea?"

"Heh-heh-heh, various local herbs."

"Have you seen the boy yet?"

"He must be still asleep. Will he like pancakes for breakfast? Tanna, would you care for pancakes?"

"Pancakes would be grand. Shouldn't we call him?"

"Oh, let him be."

"Janna, I'm uneasy about him."

Janna's eyes narrowed to slits. "All right," she said. "I wanted you to have a good breakfast first, but I suppose you have to hear. The boy is gone."

Tanna looked severely at her. "Gone? Just like that? You know more about it than you're saying."

"Yes, yes, my cats, my birds, they see everything. Just as the sun was rising, off he went through the hedge, running as fast as a young rabbit. Janna can't run that fast. And the worst of it is, he's taken my fetch-and-carry plant with him. He's a thief. Nice guest you've brought with you, Tanna Southwind. It should have been a girl anyhow."

"If he's gone, I'd better be going too."

"I wish you would stay awhile. He'll find his way, don't you think?"

"I'm uneasy."

"Well, if you must." Janna shrugged. Grandmother ate her pancake and went to pack her satchel. She glanced into the loft room and saw the huge bed with the small dent where the boy had been sleeping, and the candle that had burned only a minute or so.

Then she bade Janna good-bye. "It was fine, seeing you once more. How long it has been, hasn't it, Janna? And if anything special happens, send one of your crows, all right?"

"Good, good. I no longer belong to the association, but I still know how to crochet. I'll think of you often, Tanna Southwind."

At the woodpile Grandmother looked around once more, and they waved to each other. Then she rode on. She had to keep a sharp lookout, for the path was not very clear here. As she pumped the wheelchair handles she mumbled to herself, "I'm uneasy. Something is wrong. I feel it. But I can't do anything. It's not yet the right time."

Janna went to look for a new flowerpot for her fetch-and-carry plant. One was too big, the other too small. A third had a crack. Finally she said, "Oh, I can forget about this silly plant. I have a little boy now. That's the real thing."

Frank's mother was annoyed with Grandmother. She had spoken of spending the fall vacation with the two boys, and now off she had gone with Chris alone. Not a word had been heard from her, and when Frank hung around a bit droopily on the first day of vacation, his mother suddenly came to a decision. "How would you like me to take you to the cottage in the forest?"

Frank was at loose ends. "I don't even know if it will be any fun there," he said.

"We'll see, but I'm not going to put up with this. All year round I run Grandmother's errands. If she can take care of a stranger's child, she can take care of mine as well."

"I don't like woods all that much," Frank objected. "I prefer the ocean."

But his mother packed a big suitcase with a towel, pajamas, clean underclothes, and a heavy sweater—all things Chris had omitted taking because Grandmother had mentioned only a toothbrush. "Come, Frank, if Chris can have a nice vacation, you can too."

They took the train, and then a bus that shook and rattled over narrow roads past hayfields and wooded grooves where some trees were already colored red and yellow. The driver stopped at a rusty gate and called out, "Hazelhurst Cottages."

Frank and his mother were the only ones who got off. The gate was padlocked, but a well-tramped path showed that people usually made a detour around it. They did the same.

What a gloomy driveway it was, and what a dreary building. Not a real castle with towers and portcullises, but just a great pile of cold and forbidding brickwork. The lawn had not been cut; the driveway had become a damp path littered with withered leaves and edged on both sides by stinging nettles. There was a moldy smell in the air.

"I don't think it's very nice here," Frank said.

"Neither do I, but maybe it gets better up ahead."

Up ahead they came to the dogs. They greeted them with a volley of hoarse barking. Frank and his mother stopped and waited at the outer edge of the farmyard until at last someone came, a tall, blond farm woman. She chained the dogs and showed the two vacationers the way to the cottages. How awfully small those cottages were, but they also looked quaint with their peaked roofs. Each had its own fenced-in little garden, in which huge clumps of goldenrod and hydrangea bushes had overwhelmed the other flowers.

The farm woman had referred them to the third cottage. The door was not locked. On the counter in the kitchen stood a bowl of eggs, two unwashed cups, and a frying pan glistening with fat. There was no one there.

"They've gone into the woods without cleaning up," Mother said. "Just like her. We'll wait."

She rearranged the cushions on the bench and put a kettle of water on the stove. Frank stood at the window, looking at the dapple of sun and shadow that fell upon the path.

While Grandmother was still in the yard and totally intent on walking with her canes and on saying her good-byes to Janna, she scarcely noticed the appeals for help that Chris was sending out. But once she was trundling along in her wheelchair down a smooth path through the woods, she became very much aware of them.

By then Chris had got over the worst of his fear. He could not believe that Janna had the power she said she had. She could not make him forget the path or his home. If she didn't eat him up at once, he'd surely find a chance to escape. He was somewhat disappointed that the stone had not immediately brought Grandmother to his side, but since he had nothing else to do he went on calling her, not with his mouth but with his heart. And a feeling of his sad plight reached her soon enough. She was even able to visualize the pen in which he sat. But she did not turn back. Her awareness had a far greater reach than that of other people. She knew about things far away and in time to come. Experience had taught her to let things take their own course, especially when it was plain that the future would settle itself.

And so she continued down the path, past the white birches, the silent firs, and the gnarled oaks, where two crows were playing tag with each other. She was thinking of many things, but not for a moment of her family.

Still, she was careful not to show surprise when she found her daughter at the cottage. "So you've come to visit me, child? How nice, how nice."

"I've brought you Frank. You promised him a few days in the country," Frank's mother said reproachfully.

"So I did. Well, Frank, how does it strike you here?"

"Pretty nice, Grandmother. Where is Chris?"

"Chris is away at the moment, but he'll be back."

Frank's mother bit her lip. She was determined not to let herself be irritated by Grandmother. She began washing the cups and making coffee. "I've baked a cake for you," she said. "Frank, would you bring it out? It's in that tin box in the suitcase."

"Weren't you frightened by the dogs?" Grandmother asked.

"The farm woman chained them. Did they frighten Chris?"

"A little, I think. They're such huge beasts and jump around so, and their teeth look terribly sharp. But I don't think they're dangerous, except for somebody who comes at night and is up to no good."

"Do people like that come here?" Frank wondered. He was not at all sure he wanted to stay. It was odd that Chris was not around.

They drank coffee and ate cake. For a while it was very pleasant. Then Grandmother said, "Now I'm going to look for Chris. Will you two come along?"

"How long will it take?" Mother asked. "My bus leaves in an hour."

"It will take longer than an hour, but of course there are more buses."

"I wouldn't want to get home late."

"It's lovely weather, and nobody will mind if you come home later. But if you don't want to, that's your decision. I'm going now. Frank, put your jacket on." Grandmother hoisted herself to her feet and went toward the door as vigorously as her frailty permitted.

Frank sounded a little sulky as he said good-bye to his mother. He could not quite tell her that he really would sooner go home with her. This place didn't seem all that inviting. But maybe it would be fun, once Chris appeared. There was always something doing with Chris.

Frank's mother stayed in the cottage and busied herself washing up the coffee things. Grandmother was already speeding along the path through the woods. To Frank this forest seemed very big and very quiet. It struck him as sort of creepy. Stories of Hansel and Gretel and Little Red Riding Hood went through his mind. But of course there were no longer any witches or wolves. Foxes, yes. Would a fox bite you?

Grandmother pointed out a jay, and they heard the rat-tat-tat of a woodpecker. There were no mushrooms.

It seemed to Frank that Grandmother was taking him on an awfully long walk. When the woods thinned somewhat, they saw a few crows staring curiously down at them. For a while the birds stayed close by, but suddenly they soared up above the trees and disappeared in the distance.

At Janna's farm the geese began to cackle.

Chris was still sitting in his pigsty. Janna had brought him a cold drink. "Homemade," she said proudly. "Rhubarb punch. Try it, it's tasty. And if you give the stone back to me and promise you won't run away, I'll let you out."

"Of course I'll run away," Chris replied.

"I want to have that stone now. I need it. Maybe I'll let you go away after all."

"I won't give it up."

She glowered at him and left. Chris sniffed the punch she had brought him. He wanted it badly but did not dare drink it. Perhaps she had put something into it. Because he was afraid that the temptation would prove too great, he poured out the glass over the partition. The pig licked up the stuff at once, and Chris watched curiously to see whether the animal acted strangely or became sleepy, but he noticed nothing unusual.

What if he made a grab at Janna next time she looked in on him and took *her* prisoner? He would need something to tie her up with. He began braiding a rope of straw. But the straw made a clumsy, thick braid and was not at all strong, so he soon gave up. It really was time he did something about escaping. He'd been able to use the magic stone to cast a spell on Selina, hadn't he? Why hadn't Grandmother come? Could Janna have made a prisoner of her also? Or maybe Grandmother had intended from the start to turn him over to Janna?

He had to affect Janna's mind somehow so that she herself would set him free. But that was not so easy, for if he put into her mind Forget to lock the door, forget to lock the door, he would just be reminding her of the door. He had to give her some kind of surprise that would make her suddenly dash off, leaving the door unlocked by accident.

Chris began pondering the problem.

Janna was poking about the yard in a disgruntled state of mind. Things were not turning out at all as she had planned. She had thought that after an hour of being locked up Chris would do exactly what she wanted. All her life she had found it easy to draw people under her influence. She had never expected a child to be so obstinate.

Maybe she ought to take the stone away from him

by force. But that sort of thing was not in her nature. Janna was a witch, a real one. She radiated a kind of magnetic force that attracted animals and made people do her will. She could make anybody dance to her tune —except Chris. Here was this boy who would rather be locked up in a pigsty than have free run of the little paradise she had created on her farmstead and in the vicinity. She could not understand it at all and was deeply irked.

Disturbed in a way she had not been in years, she went about her regular chores until she noticed that the animals, and especially the birds, were becoming restless. The pigeons swooped in great circles around the house. Then the geese ran to the opening in the hedge, cackling excitedly. The chickens joined them. Finally the crows came back from the woods. With their broad wings flapping like black rags, they skimmed over the hedge, which was a sure sign for Janna that people were coming. It would be a while before they turned up, for the crows flew swiftly, but she would have to get that boy off the place before the intruders came.

Janna considered. Then she hurried to the kitchen and took down a small, round tin. It contained oatmeal cookies. With a crow on each shoulder and her black cat following her, she made for the barn. But before she crossed the threshold the birds flew up and into an elm tree, and the cat sat down on an overturned tub. With a sugary smile, her eyes almost closed amid a hundred wrinkles, Janna called out, "Chris."

No answer.

"Chris, are you there?"

Chris sat in his corner, too angry to answer. Where else would he be?

"I have some cookies here to show you that I'm your friend. But you had better give me the stone now, because otherwise I won't bring you anything more to eat."

"I can't," Chris said, "because I've swallowed it."

"That's not true."

"Come and look for it. It isn't in my pocket, and it isn't hidden in the straw. You won't find it anywhere because it's in my stomach."

Silently Janna glared at him as though her eyes could pierce him through and through. Then she turned and went away, taking the oatmeal cookies with her.

After a while Chris tried the door, and it opened. It was just as he had willed it; she had forgotten to shoot the bolt. Quietly he left the pigsty. The barn was dark inside and very high. He crept past a hay wagon. On the wall hung big black harnesses for horses. The outer door stood ajar. Chris paused there and peered through the crack before he ventured to push it open. Finally he went out. No Janna, nobody except a black cat sitting on a tub. How bright everything was outside, and how the sun shone.

The house under the trees looked like something out of a picture book, with its thatched roof, the well with the iron crank, the chickens, the geese, and the cote for the pigeons crowning it all. You'll always long for this place, Janna had said, and that was so. Even at this moment Chris was strongly tempted by it, but he resisted its lure. Nor would he ever again be so stupid as to make his getaway along the regular path. He wouldn't cross the yard, wouldn't pass by the windows. He must escape by a different route. Even if it meant wandering about in the pathless forest for days and days. Sooner or later he would have to come out into open country.

Chris stole around the barn. The way was blocked by nettles and a tangle of oak saplings. He wriggled through. Farther on, the going was somewhat better, for he came to pines with large ferns growing beneath them. The ground was covered with moss, deep green and sopping wet. He broke off a dead branch. Still, his progress was slow because he had to pick his way through underbrush. The cat followed him at some distance, and the crows, too, kept up with him, fluttering from tree to tree.

Chris suspected nothing.

CHAPTER XII

The Crows Attack

In a small village in the neighborhood of Hazelhurst Cottages a bus stopped in front of an old hotel. A strange group piled out of it. First to emerge was a tall man in a wide cape. His eyebrows were so thick that they met above his eyes, and he supervised the group's alighting from the bus with a commanding air. He was followed by a large woman, and behind her came a tiny one with a cheery, apple face. Next to hop out was a little, dark-complexioned man with high shoulders and a sharp, angular face, who looked like the clever tailor of the fairy tale. Another fairy-tale figure was an old gentleman with wavy, white hair and bright eyes that seemed to gaze far into the distance. All the rest of the party were women. The owner of the hotel counted them as they came in one by one. There were twenty-one of them.

For two days they had held meetings in their little café, meetings that stretched on deep into the night. By then the Irish sailors had long since returned to their ships, shaking their heads over those ponderous Dutchmen who talked about serious matters even in a pub.

Aside from Sybren there were quite a few others who remembered Janna and Tanna. By now it was well known that Sister Southwind had left town with Chris, and it was not hard to guess where she was bound. Only a few thought it urgent to follow them, but everyone wanted to be on the spot if something happened. And so Sister Farsight had chartered a bus that would take them all.

Doctor Onkel hung a sign in his window to tell patients he would be away. Selina put out twice her normal distribution of bird feed. Fleurtje gave extra water to her fuchsias, and Toontje just locked his door. What affairs Kiki and Amanda had to settle before leaving was not clear to any of the others, but those two were the last to appear. Then the bus could leave.

They rode east along the same highway that Chris had taken—sound asleep—in the big German trailer truck. They knew the forest where Janna lived with her crows, but they were not sure just how to reach her house. For that reason they got out at the hotel to ask the way and also to have a bite to eat after the long ride. Each member of the party ordered something different, such as chicken soup without salt, tomato juice with sugar, and buttermilk with a dash of currant liqueur. The bus driver drank nothing but a cup of coffee.

With all their different orders, they were a very troublesome group. But each of the twenty-one sorcerers was so polite and seemed so to appreciate what was done by the staff that everyone in the hotel went to special lengths to meet their wishes. The owner personally mixed the dry Martini and poured the sherry for Kiki and Amanda. His wife brought Selina a glass of lukewarm milk, and the waitresses came dancing up with clear bouillon garnished with egg yolk and chocolate milk flavored with orange peel.

The doctor asked to see a map of the neighborhood. There was one hanging in the lobby opposite the coat rack made of antlers. There on the map was marked the little castle of Hazelhurst, and behind it was a huge green area with a thin winding line running down the middle: the forest with its narrow path.

"Aren't there more roads through the woods?" the doctor asked. "And isn't there a house somewhere?"

"No," the hotelkeeper said. "Nobody lives there, and the forest is quite wild. There is never any hunting there anymore, and dead trees are not cleared away.

Ever since the last baron died mad, nobody has looked after those woods. The castle has stood empty for more than twenty years."

"Have you by any chance ever heard of Janna and her crows?"

The hotelkeeper shook his head. He consulted his wife and an old man who came there to polish the copper. They had no knowledge of a woman who lived in the woods either. But in a cupboard they found another map that showed far more detail; it was a survey map from before the Second World War. On it the thin line ran all the way through the forest and a house was marked, a farmhouse with two large barns. Deeper in the woods was another small structure, near which there had been a gravel pit. One of the waitresses had seen that pit. She came from a village on the other side of the forest.

"People said it was dangerous there," she said. "But I don't know why." She thought the road to the gravel pit must still be there. But she had never heard of Janna.

The doctor asked to borrow the map, and then the whole party crowded into the lobby to pay their individual bills and to sort out their jackets and shawls and caps. They shook hands with the hotelkeeper and the waitresses, and it took quite awhile before they had all climbed back into the bus. But at last they were ready to go again. Doctor Onkel went to sit beside the driver with the map in his hand. It was a twenty-five-minute drive before they reached a point almost directly across the forest from Hazelhurst Castle. Meanwhile, they ate the sandwiches they had brought with them in paper bags.

The road was there, but the driver would not venture on it. "This bus isn't made for roads like that, and that road isn't made for a bus," he said. "Maybe a truck could do it. A road like that goes more and more to pieces the farther in you go. And I'll have no room to turn around."

"But these old people can't walk so far. Try it just a little way. Let's drive in as far as you can."

The driver finally was persuaded to turn into the road. He forged ahead a few yards, then another few yards.

"Look," Doctor Onkel said, "up ahead there is a place where you can surely turn around."

So the driver drove on a little ways farther. That's how things go with witches on board. He himself soon began enjoying the challenge as he eased his bus through the washouts and deep furrows in the road. It wound among magnificent old beeches, then across a heath of scattered pines, birches, and blackthorn. After about a quarter of an hour they reached the gravel pit, which was a series of deep excavations in yellow sand rimmed by crooked trees whose naked roots clung to the sheer walls.

"This is where I stop," the driver announced, and everyone understood, for the road disappeared completely. But there was a large level area where three buses could easily turn around.

The doctor alighted first and studied the map. "The house must be close by," he said. "And look over there. We're on the right trail. Crows."

The passengers, who got off the bus slowly and cautiously, saw four large oak trees. Half of their branches were dead, but a tangle of gnarled sprouts grew from the trunks. And in the trees perched dozens of crows uttering sinister cries.

The driver was the only person who remained in the bus. He began attacking his sandwiches, and he threw a crust toward the birds, but not one swooped down for it. They began flying around in great arcs that grew steadily smaller until, fluttering and screeching, they were hurling themselves straight at the windowpanes of the bus. That was a little too much for the driver. "When will you want to leave here?" he called out to the doctor.

"In a couple of hours."

"OK."

Swaying, the bus drove off. The crows remained.

* * *

Meanwhile, Grandmother and Frank had reached Janna's house. At first they saw no one. But they heard a splashing sound that came from one of the two barns and made for it. Janna was thumping a thick stick up and down in a barrel. She was churning butter. Stiffly she nodded to her guests but did not stop working.

"We've come for Chris," Grandmother said.

"He ran away. I told you so this morning."

"Yes, but that wasn't true."

Janna shrugged. "He isn't here."

"We'll look for him."

Janna cast a scornful look at Grandmother's wheelchair, but she said nothing more. Janna knew quite well that she had not locked the door of the pigsty, and she thought that Chris must be far away by now.

Grandmother drove herself around the yard, deep in thought. "Frank," she said after a while, "you have to take a look in this barn."

"It's so dark in there," Frank said.

"It won't seem so bad once you're inside."

Hesitantly Frank went in through the low door. He saw the big hay wagon and the hard leather straps and halter on the wall. Step by step he went deeper into the barn.

Chris had tried to make the most distance he could. He had crawled through prickly brambles and pressed his way through the sharp needles of pine saplings until he suddenly came upon a narrow path. There he began to run, frequently bending to avoid low branches. The path ended in a level open field where grass and heather grew. In it stood a small, low building, another barn, and near it three sheep.

The barn door was open, and since he was out of breath, Chris went in. Quite possibly this barn also belonged to Janna's farm, but he had to rest, and the structure was so tumbledown that there were plenty of cracks, so that he could see anyone who came along.

Chris peered in all directions through the holes and cracks. Behind the barn there was another sheep. In front and on the right was the open field, and on the left he saw four tall oaks, misshapen from age, or perhaps from the large numbers of crows that lived in them and let their droppings fall to the ground. He could not see any farther than the trees because of the many oak saplings growing around them, but perhaps there was some kind of road beyond them, for he thought he heard the sound of a motor. Chris listened intently, but all he could hear now were the cries of the birds, hoarse and threatening.

The crows were all descended from the ones that Janna had trained for the circus many years ago. The cleverest of them stayed with her almost all the time. They understood her so well that they could carry messages, but the others had also learned a great deal from her. Janna did not like surprise visitors. If anybody came by the long way, the winding path from Hazelhurst, the animals always warned her. But that seldom happened, for the tourists who rented the cottages during the summer usually took only very short walks in the woods. They preferred going to look at villages in the vicinity or swimming in the pond. People who came from the other side and crossed the heath did not like to pass by the big black birds that so obviously dominated the area and let it be known with raucous voices. If someone did venture into the woods and found the little path, the crows would attack. Once they had chased a fourteen-year-old boy until he fell into the deepest of the gravel pits. And a poacher had been so battered by their hard beaks that he never wandered in that direction again. Neither the boy nor the poacher had been willing to tell exactly what had happened to them. But since that time the abandoned gravel pit had been called a dangerous place, and even fewer persons came out that way.

After Chris felt somewhat rested, he decided to go on. He refused to be frightened by the screeching of the birds but left the sheep shed and walked around the clump of oak trees. There he came upon a fearful sight. Ahead were far more crows than he had seen in the trees. Hundreds of them were flying around in

close circles, scolding continually, "Caw-caw-caw-caw caw-caw." A small band of people stood huddled close together, unable to move because the crows attacked furiously if any of them took so much as a step. Selina stood there waving her arms. She was used to dealing with birds and was now trying to impose her will on them. In fact, it did seem that the crows gave her a wider berth than the others. But otherwise, what she was doing had no effect. The group of sorcerers at that moment looked rather like a bunch of miserable, terror-stricken boobies.

The scene made Chris furiously angry. "You ugly birds," he screamed at them, "go away!"

But of course they did nothing of the kind. It was striking that not a single crow attacked him, even when he came very close to the group. That was because Janna had sent her two favorite birds to accompany him. They were charged to watch where he was going, but also to see that nothing happened to him. Chris did not realize this and thought he was keeping the birds off with his own courage, as had been the case with the dogs at the farmhouse.

"You mustn't be afraid," he told the people. "If you show no fear, they won't bother you."

But this advice did not change the situation.

"Couldn't you report this to this Janna person?"

Doctor Onkel asked. "She's the one who has bewitched these birds. I think she is the only one who can call them off."

Report to Janna? Chris looked aghast. But of course the doctor couldn't know that Janna had locked him up in a pigsty and that he was now escaping. He certainly couldn't go back, could he? But that shouldn't be necessary anyhow. All these people were witches and sorcerers themselves. It mightn't hurt them at all to see that magic wasn't always such fun.

He saw the way the two glamorous ladies ducked nervously as another huge black bird zoomed toward them. There was also an old white-haired man, who looked around rather absently, and the friendly cobbler, and a very nice, droll-looking little woman. Once again Chris felt sorry for them. Maybe they were all wicked witches, but it would be unfortunate if a crow hacked out someone's eye.

"All right," Chris said, "I guess I'll go and tell her what a wicked old woman she is." He ran off, and none of the birds interfered with him.

It occurred to him that he could shout at Janna from a distance, telling her what he thought of her and her witchcraft. He would be mighty careful not to let her get hold of him again.

Just as he had thought, the narrow path led to the farmstead. Cautiously he walked into the yard, keeping a sharp lookout in all directions. Then he caught sight of Grandmother in her wheelchair. "Grand-mother!"

"Hello, Chris, lucky you're here. We were just looking for you."

"I was locked up. Janna stuck me into a pigsty, but I escaped. I called with the stone all the time, but it didn't work."

"I was aware of it, but I had other things to do. And I thought, Chris can rescue himself. But now I'm here."

"It's true," Chris said proudly. "I did rescue myself."

Frank came out of the barn. He was holding the braided straw that Chris had intended to tie up Janna with.

"Hello, Frank. I was shut up in a pigsty, and Janna kept bringing me things to eat all the time. She's a wicked witch, you know."

At that point Janna joined them. "And you are a thief. You stole my stone and my fetch-and-carry plant."

"*My* stone," Chris said.

"Actually," Grandmother said, "the stone is still mine."

"What stone?" Frank asked.

"I found it in Grandmother's wheelchair when we went for a ride in it."

"You didn't have to go blabbing about that," Frank said, his face red, but Grandmother only laughed.

"I've been wondering how you got hold of it."

"So! That proves it! Now do you see what a thief he is?" Janna blustered. "He even stole Tanna's wheelchair."

"But I'm not a wicked witch! Back there in the woods there must be a thousand bewitched crows that are hacking away at people. You have to put a stop to it."

"I called them off long ago," Janna said. "As soon as I knew you were coming back here. But I'll bet those idiots haven't even noticed yet that the crows are gone."

"Good afternoon, dear friends." Doctor Onkel appeared from behind the barn. He was followed by Selina, Toontje, and the rest. "Good afternoon," they chorused.

Janna stamped her foot in her rage. "What are you doing here? I sent the crows away, but that doesn't mean that you're welcome."

The old man came up to her. "Janna, why Janna, is it you?"

She calmed down somewhat. "Well, well, Sybren, what an old face you've got now."

Sybren bent his venerable head so as not to look straight at Janna's toothless mouth and thin, straggling hair. She had as cruel a tongue as she had had years ago, and he was as helpless against her spite as ever.

Chris went over to Grandmother's wheelchair. "Should we leave?"

"No," Grandmother said. "We're going to fight this out here and now, and remember that you're fighting along with me. Use the stone. You can do it." She whispered so vehemently that it sounded like hissing.

"We have come," Doctor Onkel said, "to settle a matter of great importance to the world. All of us know that it concerns the precious object that for so long was in the possession of our respected Sister Southwind. The last I heard, it was taken by a crow. Is that correct? And where is the object now?"

For a moment there was silence. Then Chris took a step forward. "Here," he said, taking the magic stone from his pocket and holding it out so that all could see it. "I wanted to give it back to Grandmother, but she no longer wants it. I no longer want it either, because it is a bad thing. Much too much fuss has been made about it. So it's better that nobody should have it. I'm going to throw it into the well."

He started toward the well, but he did not get far. Three or four pairs of hands seized him. Grandmother began to laugh, and Janna cried out in her shrill voice, "He's a thief and a liar too. He said he'd swallowed it."

One hand after the other released Chris. Selina gazed

with avid eyes at the stone, which he still held in his palm. Fleurtje began fumbling with the hearing-aid switch in her bosom. She could not make out anything of what was going on.

Suddenly Sybren collapsed. He had been leaning heavily on Amanda for quite a while. "I'm done in. I must sit down for a moment."

Doctor Onkel and Madame Farsight rushed over to him. They half carried him a short distance away where he could sit leaning against a tree.

Little Toontje spoke up. "Would you mind if we came in for a bit so we can rest up?"

Janna threw her door wide open. "Come right in. Come into Janna's house, all of you. You can have linden-blossom tea and oatmeal cookies, and if you want to talk things over I'll leave, since I no longer belong to the Fine Thread Association."

"You certainly do belong," Grandmother said. "Here you belong. I intend to speak, and Fleurtje, put that thing in your ear because you must know what is being said."

Sybren was helped into the house. The others followed, Grandmother last. "Come along!" she said to Chris. But he did not want to. Whereupon she said to him once more, "Use it!"

CHAPTER XIII

More Needlework

Chris and Frank stayed outside. Once all the people were out of the way, chickens came tripping back to the farmyard. They clucked, the pigeons cooed, and from the chestnut tree came the soft fluting notes of a songbird.

"It's nice here," Frank said.

"Yes," Chris said, "I thought so too, but not when I was shut up in the pigsty."

"What had you done to be punished like that?"

"Taken the magic stone, but it wasn't even hers. And I also took a plant, a dried-up stalk, that she'd bewitched."

"That can't be. There's no such thing as bewitching."

"There is so. Your own grandmother is a witch."

"It's not true. There are no witches. My mother says so."

"So does mine, but I don't care what mothers say. I know what I've seen, and I'll do whatever I like."

Frank said no more. They strolled around.

"They have a cow here with real milk in her," Chris boasted. "Super, isn't it? And if Janna and I weren't mad at each other, she would have taught me how to milk."

"I don't like milk from a cow," Frank said.

"All milk comes from cows."

"No, it doesn't. Haven't you heard of milk factories?"

"Yes." Suddenly Chris was no longer so sure. "They chew their cuds, too," he said quickly. "Want to see?"

He led the way to the pasture where the cow stood stolidly, her jaws grinding away, a mucousy green string hanging from her mouth. The pink udder was swollen with milk.

They stood reverently watching for a while. Then Chris said, "Want me to prove that witchcraft is real? You watch, I'll bewitch the cow. I can do it, but it may take me a while."

Grandmother had said, "Use the stone." He had understood what she meant: that he should influence the group so that the decision would be that he could keep the stone. But he did not feel the slightest desire to use the stone that way. His idea would be more fun. With the stone in his hand he looked at the cow. First he imagined what it was like to be a cow, with half-digested grass in one's mouth. The cow brought up another cud, and Chris belched. He was no longer thinking of Frank at all. He almost forgot that he wanted to make the cow do something, but then she took a step forward. Chris felt the step inside himself, and then another and another. It was working; he was making the cow go where he wished. A little faster, come on now, get going. The cow began to trot. The green string lengthened, broke, and was sucked back into the mouth. Her udder swayed. At a spot where the barbed wire was loose Chris pulled it down, and *whoosh* over she bounded. With thudding hooves she ran down the path to the spot to which Chris was directing her: the window of Janna's living room. She bent her head and caught her horns under the window. With a clatter, the window went up. The cow stuck her whole head into the room and went "Moo!"

It had taken quite a while before everyone found a seat. Janna did not have twenty-one chairs. They brought in cushions and the mattress stuffed with fresh fern. Doctor Onkel rushed about arranging things, and Janna muttered, "Meetings! In my day we didn't bother with them, and the men didn't have so much say."

Still, she passed around a platter of oatmeal cookies and was visibly pleased when everyone admired her big crocheted lampshade.

At last everyone had a seat.

Doctor Onkel said, "Ahem."

Grandmother said, "Now. . . ."

They both wanted to be first to have the floor and cast annoyed looks at each other. Then the window flew up with a crash, and the big bovine head said, "Moo!"

A few of those who sat close by jumped with fright. A few others shook their heads indignantly. But most of them were greatly amused.

"That brat," Janna said. "He's bewitched my Bessie."

Bessie gave another long, loud moo. Then she drew her head back, her horns tearing a triangle out of the curtain. Janna ran out.

"This is an outrage," Doctor Onkel said. "Isn't it clear that this cannot go on any longer?"

"Oh," Kiki said, "it doesn't strike me as all that terrible."

"It *is* bad," Selina commented. "The child does not realize what he has hold of."

"He certainly does," Toontje said. "He's handling it very well."

Grandmother said not a word. She sat in her wheelchair, a tiny figure, and looked at each of the others in turn.

"Dear friends," the doctor began. "Let us settle this matter right now. Is there anyone here who is still not convinced that the problem must be grappled with?"

"But what exactly is the problem?" Fleurtje asked. "I simply don't understand anything anymore."

Selina explained, "We don't want a small boy to have the magic stone."

"But he's already had it for quite some time. I myself crocheted the pattern that told you all about it."

"So he has. But we don't think it is good. That was what we were discussing at such length day before yesterday. You were there yourself."

"Oh," Fleurtje said, "I didn't follow it very well. I'm sorry. But I still don't understand it. The boy is certainly one of us, isn't he? Surely all of you can feel that, can't you? He is the one who will possess the stone later. That's perfectly plain. I'm certainly not the only one of us who can see into the future, am I?"

"No, Fleurtje," Grandmother said. "I can too. And do you think," she asked, suddenly sitting up straight and pounding the floor with her cane, "that I enjoyed parting with the stone? Do you think I didn't try to get it back? But this little fellow from the start had the strength to resist me. Me!" She gave another thump with her cane. "Not one of you has ever been able to do that."

"Dear Sister Southwind," Doctor Onkel said, "we

sympathize. But the fact is that in advanced age one's forces weaken. It is also true that in youth one does not always have control of his forces. I am still of the opinion that this precious object should not be entrusted to a child."

"Do you think a child has no brains? You're mistaken, my dear man. If you cannot trust someone when he is young, you cannot trust him later either. I can see what a person has in him and what will become of him. And you, Selina, can do the same. If your greed were not greater than your honesty, you would have recognized long ago that the boy is destined to receive the stone. But you didn't want that to happen. Your will blocked off your insight."

"That's true," Selina replied shamefacedly.

"And there is something else," Grandmother went on, somewhat more mildly. "He has never done anything wrongful with it. He understands the danger of the stone better than all of you. And for that reason he is already the most suitable person to have it."

"But still he's a thief," grumbled Janna, who had just returned.

"And what about yourself?" Grandmother asked. "How did you come to have it anyhow? You say that Chris stole it from you, but it was never yours."

"Sisters, dear sisters," the doctor implored.

"I'm not your dear sister," Janna said acidly, "and

you talk too much, as I said before. No doubt about it, you went to school too long. People learn all the wrong things in the schools. I know, because I sat in them myself once upon a time. I did not steal the stone. I sent the crow to Tanna with a message that she was welcome. Not to seize the stone; I can swear to that. But the crow had it with him when he returned. So I thought that Tanna had given it to him, but she said nothing about it and neither did I. I had hidden it in the rain barrel. I thought, If it's meant for the child, let him find it. But that might have taken a long time. In the meanwhile, he could have grown up here. That would have been nice. Because when you deal with trees and bees, you learn better things than you learn at school. Those educators think they know what the world is all about, but they're hopelessly wrong, because the world is different every day. Things are always growing and changing. And now they've changed to the point that Chris found the stone in the rain barrel in less than an hour instead of in a year. That made me kind of cross, especially because he isn't a girl. But by now it ought to be plain as the nose on your face that the magic stone belongs to him. If you members of the Fine Thread Association can't see that, you've gone downhill a long way."

"You know, Janna," Sybren hazarded, "if it's all right with you maybe we might come out here now and then. Do us good to get close to the soil again."

"Well, that's up to you. But I wouldn't want the whole gang of you at once."

"Well, there's no doubt what the membership has decided," the doctor said. "I haven't gone downhill so far that I cannot feel it. But still, how I will blame myself if the boy does harm!"

And then Chris's own head came through the open window, and he said, "I won't do any harm because I'm not going to use the stone. I'm against witchcraft."

Earlier, when Janna came rushing out, Chris still felt so much like a cow that he stood still, but Frank dragged him out of the way and they hid behind the chicken coop. They heard Janna grumbling, "That brat. Bessie could easily have torn her udder."

The boys did not take that warning very seriously, for there was no sign of a wound of any kind on Bessie. She went back to her grazing as if nothing had happened, and after Janna returned indoors the boys almost of their own accord went to the window that the cow had opened. They could hear the voices plainly, especially while Janna was giving her little lecture, so they sat on the ground with their backs against the wall and listened.

But Chris could not resist putting his oar in when the doctor alluded to the possibility of his doing harm.

And so he spoke up loud and clear, right in the faces of all those experts in witchery. "I'm against witchcraft." But no one took offense. They laughed, all of them, even Janna and Selina.

"The water is boiling," Janna cried out. "I'm going to make tea. What kind would you like? A brew to make you merry, or would you rather have one that goes a bit to your heads?"

"We would like tea from the herbs that grow around the place."

"That kind makes you sleepy," Chris said. "And it gives the tables and chairs bright edges."

"All kinds of herbs grow here. You have a lot to learn, you rascal."

"We must get back to the bus," the doctor said. "I think it must be waiting for us at the gravel pit by now. If the crows haven't frightened off the driver."

"Lucky he has something new to worry about," Janna said. "Tea first." She poured her brew into cups, glasses, bowls, and jars. All sipped it with enjoyment, but hurriedly. Then they took their leave.

"Thank you, Grandmother Tanna," Selina said. "Again I know myself a little better."

Chris and Frank walked the others back to the bus, which was waiting near the oak trees. Amanda gave each of the boys a kiss. Selina invited them to her studio; she said she wanted to draw them. Fleurtje told their fortunes. "There are riches waiting for Frank when he grows up," she said. "But not for Chris."

"That can't be so," Chris objected. "I made up my mind long ago that I'm going to be rich."

"I know that, but in the course of your life you're going to have to choose many times, not just once, and you'll always make the choice that keeps you from being rich. But you'll never regret the choice, so it won't matter."

The two boys waved as the bus drove off. The crows circled over it, dipping and swooping, for a part of the way. When the crows wheeled around again, the boys started back to the farm.

They stayed there the rest of the week, and there was no more talk about the stone, the pigsty, or witchcraft. Until one day Chris found the fetch-and-carry plant. It was lying on the ground in a corner of the yard, completely withered and dry. Sadly Chris brought it to Janna.

"I wanted to take care of it, give it water and horse manure, but now it's dead."

"It wasn't a living plant," Janna explained. "I had practiced making things move, and this stalk was flexible and could be easily kept in balance because of its five roots. There were lots of things I could do with it, but it was just a trick. And now I've stopped doing such tricks because I've decided I want to be a member of the association again. They don't like you to do tricks for your own pleasure or just for a performance."

And then the conversation turned to the magic stone after all. For Chris was still worrying whether it was good or bad to use it. Grandmother said, "Nothing is ever just good or just bad. It's always a little of both, or it's good for some and bad for others."

"But then how are you going to know what you ought to do?"

"You never know for certain," Janna said. "People know for certain only in the schools, and there they turn you into a fool. The teacher says, 'One is one, and it's always the same.' There never was such nonsense. One dollar you've worked for is a lot different from one you've stolen. And a dollar for you is not the same as one for a rich man. Two apples can look exactly the same, but there'll be a worm inside one. Then the teacher says, 'Divide the apple into four equal parts.' Idiocy. The parts are never equal, and the child whose eyes are bigger than his stomach always thinks he's been given the smallest part. I tell you, school is good for nothing. You'd do better to leave the boy here, Tanna Southwind."

"Out of the question," Grandmother said. "He has to go back to his mother, and if he learns a few wrong-headed things, that's no harm. Do you have a crochet hook and some thread? And could one of your crows carry a message to Germany?"

"Certainly, certainly." Janna hurried over to a chest and took out a round tin box. She opened it and handed Grandmother a ball of fine black yarn.

"Chris, will you come and watch? We're going to crochet a collar for a crow."

Frank also came over to look, but soon lost interest and went outside. Chris paid close attention to Grandmother.

"We always make a row of chain stitches when we want to mention a particular day. So and so many stitches mean so and so many days after the new moon, and if the intended time is twelve o'clock you do one row of twelve inside. Sometimes it turns out to be just a simple loop—when, for instance, your date falls on the first day of the new moon. For afternoon hours we run our row backwards. A certain place is indicated by tight stitches. I can't teach you all that at once, because you first have to know the positions of the stars. Long stitches indicate movement. Right now I'm making long stitches in the direction of the place where we are now, followed by other long stitches in the direction of home.

When the driver of the truck that brought us here receives this needlework, he'll know that we would like to ride back with him on Saturday. There, look at that. And now, of course, we have to add at the end, Regards from Tanna and Janna. I make a scalloped edge around the whole thing and then our special signs, which we've decided for ourselves. Janna has a crow's foot, and I have a small, five-pointed star."

Chris could not imagine that a truck driver would ever be able to read such messages, but the crow collar was certainly a pretty little thing. "I don't know whether I'll ever learn to send letters like that," he said. "It kind of reminds me of the spider web above the kitchen door. That looks altogether different from the webs of other spiders."

"A spider web? I must see it!" both women exclaimed at once.

Of course Janna got to it first. "Sure enough, Tanna. There's a weaver spider here. Mihaela has sent me a message."

"What does it say?"

A spider black as pitch sat in the corner of a peculiar web above the kitchen door. The web had no one center; there were five different centers and many crisscrossing threads. Two fat flies had already been caught in the web and were completely wrapped up. For that reason

Grandmother and Janna could not properly read the message. Janna shook the spider into a matchbox and released it in a large glass jar. There it immediately began weaving a new web. They left it alone until after they had eaten, and by then the message was plain.

"Mihaela wants to see the boy who has the magic stone," Janna said. "She already knows about it. She knows he's not a girl, and she wants to see him. Chris, Mihaela wants to see you!"

"Who is Mihaela?" Chris asked.

"She is the most distinguished woman in our association," Grandmother said. "It's a very special experience to meet her. Long ago I once went to see her. She is blind."

"Then she can't very well see me."

"Yes, she can, in her way. You must go there."

"All right," Chris said. "Where does she live?"

"In Rumania, near a small river that's called the Olt or the Alt. I don't remember exactly anymore, but when you're there you'll find her of your own accord."

"Way off in Rumania! But how will I get there? I'll never be anywhere near it."

"Oh, it doesn't have to be right away. You'll find an opportunity sooner or later."

Chris did not believe it. Maybe when I'm twenty-one, he thought, which was so far in the future it was as

good as never. But still he liked to think that such an important woman so far away knew about him, and he kept going to look at the big black spider, which had been released again and was now weaving a web on the barn, a web of the same pattern.

"Mihaela has thousands of those spiders," Grandmother told him.

The truck driver actually received the needlework and understood it, for at the agreed time—after Frank and Chris had trundled Grandmother the long way through the woods to the rusty gate of Hazelhurst—they heard a thundering noise in the distance. The truck pulled up at the gate. The jack was fetched from the back, and Grandmother was lifted to the cab. Frank had not seen this process before and was much impressed.

The cab was big enough for four, and this time Chris did not fall asleep.

They dropped Chris off at his house just as his father came home. Father had been examining the sand samples from his last expedition, and he showed Chris two cupfuls of the teeth of animals that had lived a million years or so ago.

"Next year I'll have to go out of the country to do a study," he said. "Perhaps I can arrange it so that all of you can come along, because it should be a beautiful trip. We might go during the Easter recess. I have to do some work at a river in Rumania."

"Is the name of the river the Alt?" Chris asked.

"Yes, the Alt or the Olt. How did you know that?"

"Oh," Chris said, "I just happen to know certain things. That's great spider country."